MANUEL MARTIN

THE DREAMER WHO
THE SECRETS OF THE UNIVERSE...

Book III

War of the Gods

ILLUSTRATED BY MARK H. GOLDING

SECOND EDITION
September 2020

ISBN: 9798698342908

Alexandria Library Publishing House

alexlib.com

Cover design by Mark H. Golding
Colorist: Sajid Black

FIRST EDITION

Published by Vantage Press, Inc.
516 Wesrt 34th Street, New York, New York 10001

ISBN: 978-0-9749196-5-2

Writer:
Manuel Martinez

Illustrator:
Mark H. Golding

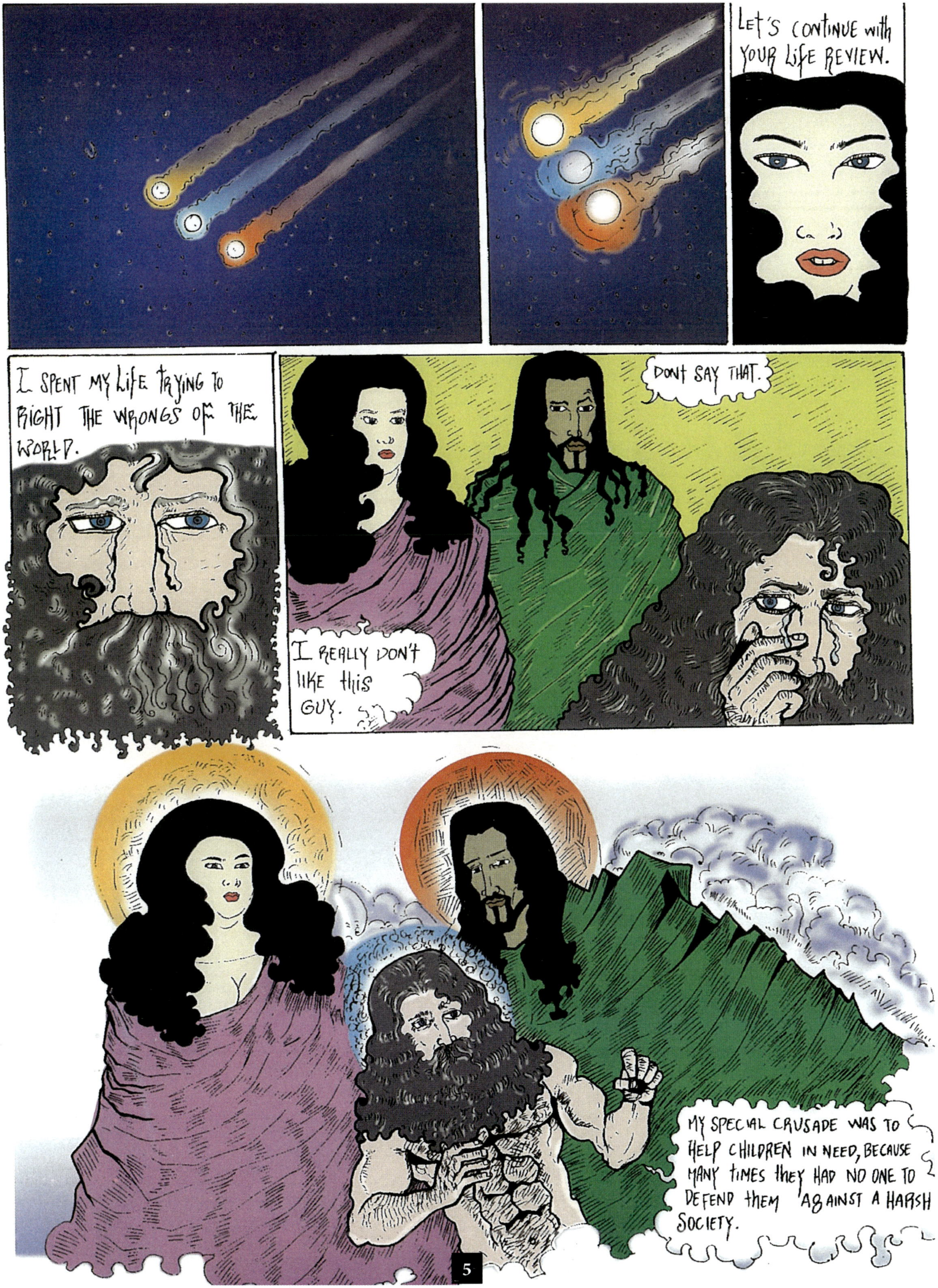

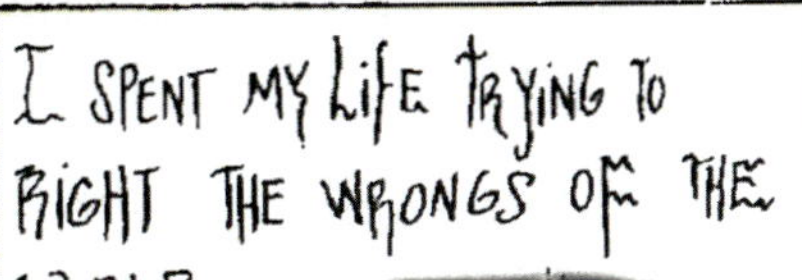

MY SPECIAL CRUSADE WAS TO HELP CHILDREN IN NEED, BECAUSE MANY TIMES THEY HAD NO ONE TO DEFEND THEM AGAINST A HARSH SOCIETY.

I REMEMBER WHEN I RECEIVED A LETTER FROM ELOISE, A TWENTY-ONE-YEAR-OLD GIRL THAT HAD BEEN IN PRISON SINCE SHE WAS FOURTEEN YEARS OLD. SHE HAD READ ONE OF MY BOOKS ABOUT REINCARNATION AND PAST LIVES, AND SHE BEGGED ME TO VISIT HER SO WE COULD TALK.
DID YOU?!!
WHENEVER I RECEIVED A REQUEST TO SPEAK TO SOMEONE IN NEED, MY SOUL RESPONDED TO THE MESSAGE.
I BELIEVE I WAS ON EARTH TO LIVE COURAGEOUSLY AGAINST ALL ODDS, AND TO MAKE CHANGES THAT WOULD BENEFIT MANKIND.
TELL US MORE ABOUT ELOISE.

THE MIAMI HERALD HAD PRINTED SEVERAL ARTICLES ABOUT ELOISE'S CASE, AND SHE MAILED THEM TO ME SO THAT I WOULD BE AWARE OF THE FACTS THAT LED TO HER PRESENT SITUATION.
MIAMI HERALD
Eloise WAS JUST A CHILD WHEN SHE WAS TRIED AS AN ADULT, AND SENTENCED LIKE AN ADULT.
JAIL
I'M LISTENING....
NELLY
Eloise
AT THE AGE OF THIRTEEN ELOISE WAS A TYPICAL TEENAGER. SHE WAS INTERESTED IN FUNKY clothes AND PLASTIC BARRETTES FOR HER HAIR. HER PARENTS AND GRANDPARENTS ADORED HER.

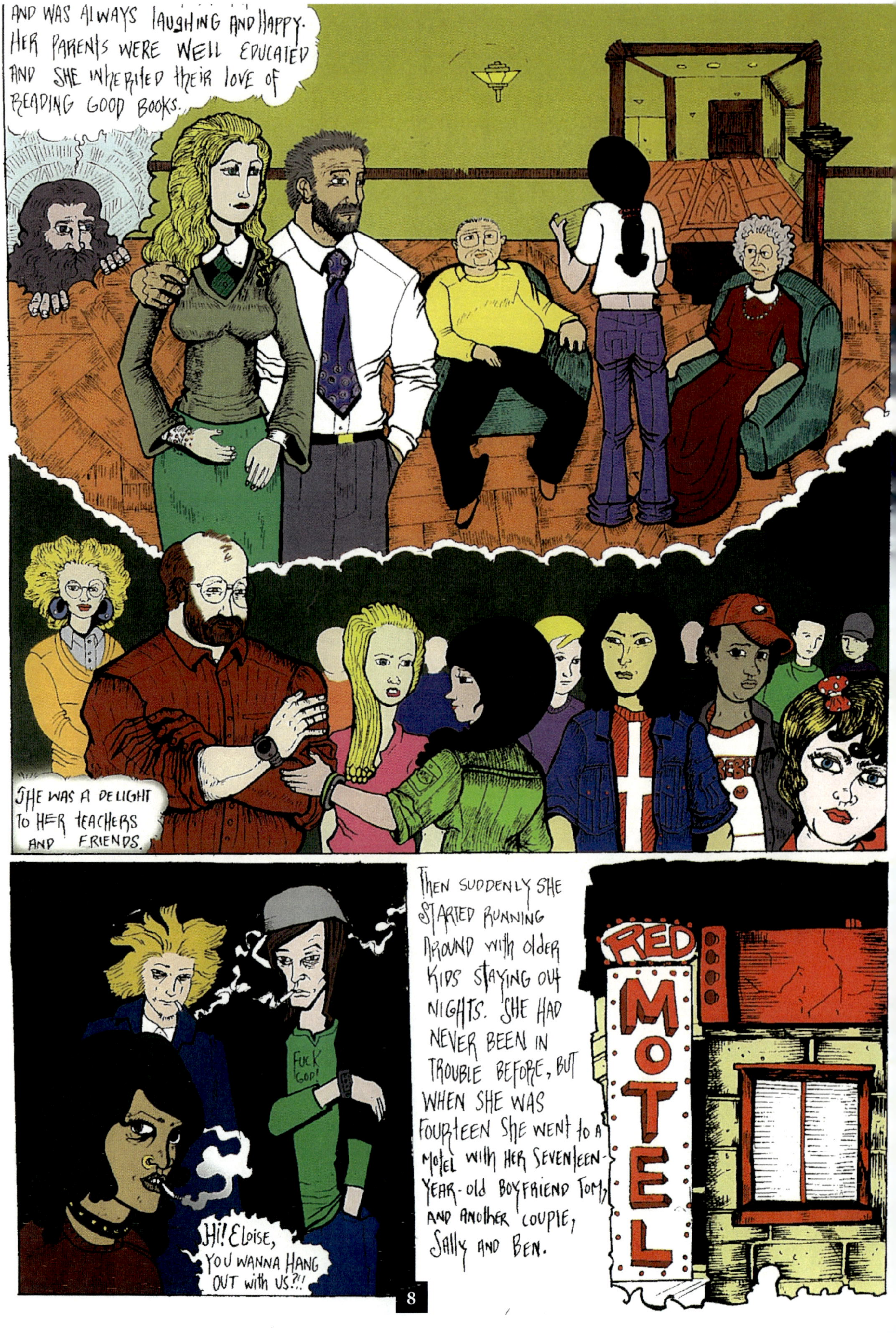

AND WAS ALWAYS LAUGHING AND HAPPY. HER PARENTS WERE WELL EDUCATED AND SHE INHERITED THEIR LOVE OF READING GOOD BOOKS.

SHE WAS A DELIGHT TO HER TEACHERS AND FRIENDS.

THEN SUDDENLY SHE STARTED RUNNING AROUND WITH OLDER KIDS STAYING OUT NIGHTS. SHE HAD NEVER BEEN IN TROUBLE BEFORE, BUT WHEN SHE WAS FOURTEEN SHE WENT TO A MOTEL WITH HER SEVENTEEN-YEAR-OLD BOYFRIEND TOM, AND ANOTHER COUPLE, SALLY AND BEN.

RED MOTEL
VACANCY
What happened at the motel?
When Eloise and Sally were sitting in the lobby drinking Coca colas, a forty-five year old man, Edward approached them and offered to take them out to a movie later that evening. The girls told him to come to their motel room at seven p.m. When he arrived Tom and Ben were waiting for him.

While Eloise and Sally watched.
They Beat Him to Death with a Bat,
Instead of calling the Police to report a murder, Eloise went along with the others to the dead man's House, and Helped rob it. She was in Shock after witnessing the Brutal Killing.

They were all caught and Eloise was given a fourteen-year prison term for second degree murder.
She got what she deserved and you know that Sebastian. You should have told her. it was the law of karma.
SWAT
Get there ass... up in that truck!
SWAT
SWAT
SWAT
SWAT
SWAT
SWAT
SWAT
I know that but Eloise had gone from an immature teenager to an immature young woman in those seven long years.
I was wrong taking part in the crime, I swear I would never do that if I had the chance again.
PRISON

HER PARENTS STILL VISITED WITH HER AND SENT HER BOOKS.
THEY WORKED CLOSELY WITH DIFFERENT LAWYERS AND SOME AUTHORITIES TO APPEAL HER SENTENCES. BUT SHE BECAME VERY DEPRESSED BY THE TERRIBLE ENVIRONMENT AND CRUELTY WITHIN THE PRISON.
YOU GON BE MY B TONIGH GOT PROB WITH THA
NO

She was transferred many times to other prisons because of allegations of sexual abuse that were being investigated at the jails she was in. In one of the prisons she was groped by a prison guard b was afraid to tell anyone because she knew she would be punished if she said anything, and she thought no one would believe he Eloise knew she would be getting out of prison in seven years, but she feared the future. Her education had stopped at the time she went to jail.
FELLAS... AKE AN EXAMPIE THIS HERE .... HEN WHORE.... H.. YEAH!
AHHHH! FUCKIN.. BITCH,... BIT ME !!!
HA HA HA HA HA HA HA HA HA

Rapist!
WHEN HER FATHER ASKED ABOUT THAT, HE WAS TOLD THAT THE STATE PRISON SYSTEM IS NOT GEARED TOWARDS EDUCATION, AND DOES NOT OFFER REHABILITATION TO OFFENDERS THAT ARE NOT PART OF THE JUVENILE SYSTEM.
So Eloise had given up ALL HOPE FOR ANY KIND OF NORMAL FUTURE. HER APPEAL TO SEE ME WAS A DESPERATE CALL FOR HELP.
DID YOU HE HER?

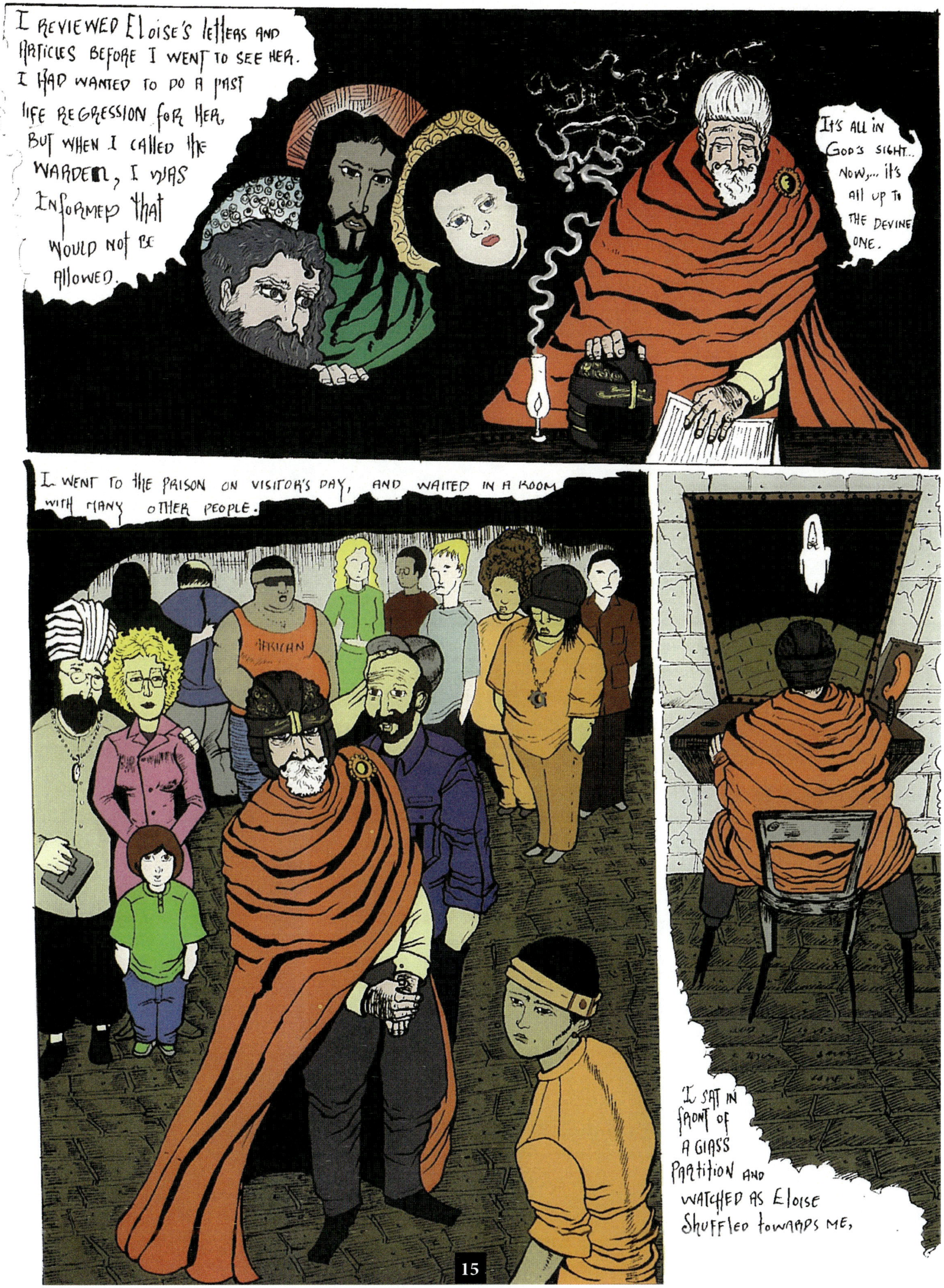

I REVIEWED Eloise's letters AND ARTICLES BEFORE I WENT TO SEE HER. I HAD WANTED TO DO A PAST LIFE REGRESSION FOR HER, BUT WHEN I CALLED THE WARDEN, I WAS INFORMED THAT WOULD NOT BE ALLOWED.

It's ALL IN GOD'S SIGHT... NOW,... it's ALL UP TO THE DEVINE ONE.

I WENT TO THE PRISON ON VISITOR'S DAY, AND WAITED IN A ROOM WITH MANY OTHER PEOPLE.

AFRICAN

HER HEAD BENT AND HER EYES looking DOWN. She SAT ON the CHAIR, facing ME, ON the opposite SIDE of the GLASS,

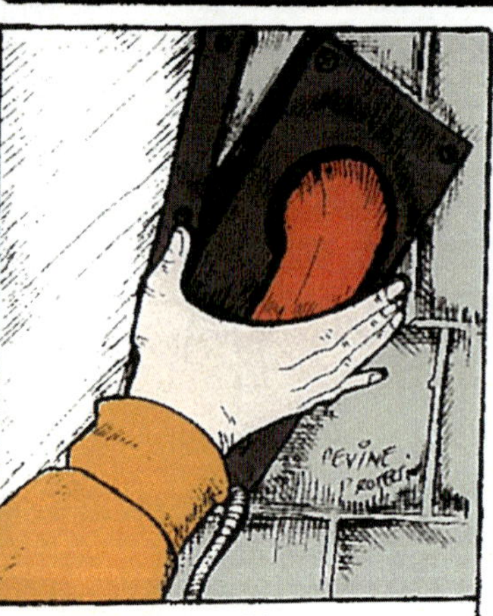

AND PICKED UP THE PHONE, I PRAYED FOR STRENGTH AND THE RIGHT WORDS TO SAY TO HER.

AS A PHYSICIAN I KNEW THE IMPORTANCE OF MIND, BODY AND SOUL WORKING IN UNITY, AND I SAW the PAIN THAT SHE WAS IN.

Hello, DR. CAMOTE, AND thanks for coming to see ME. I READ YOUR BOOKS, AND I thought you might BE ABLE to help ME, BECAUSE NO ONE ELSE CAN.

LET ME TRY TO EXPLAIN. BEFORE WE ARE REINCARNATED WE ARE IN THE WAITING PLACE, AND OUR SPIRITUAL GUIDES REVIEW OUR PAST LIFE WITH US.

OUR DEEDS AND ACTIONS AND WORDS ARE JUDGED, AND AFTER WE ARE EVALUATED, WE FIND OUT WHAT WE NEED TO CORRECT WHEN WE RETURN TO EARTH IN THE FUTURE.

THIS IS JUST ONE LIFETIME, AND YOU WILL HAVE MANY MORE. BE CAREFUL OF THE WORDS YOU SPEAK, BECAUSE THEY HAVE LIFE. EVEN IF EVERYONE ELSE AROUND YOU DISPLAYS CRUELTY, GO SOFTLY WITH KINDNESS. EVEN IF EVERYONE ELSE DISPLAYS HATE, RETURN IT WITH LOVE. TIME GOES SWIFTLY AND IN SEVEN MORE YEARS YOU WILL BE OUT OF HERE.

God has given you a mission in life, and you must meditate and ask yourself to find out what that mission is. Find your dream and reach for it.
It is not too late to wake up and go after the impossible.
I want to thank you all for doing a great job..... without you there is no me... you all contributed to the vision of the Eloise Design Fashion Collection.
Times up!
Thank you Dr. Camote. will you come to see me again?
Yes, I will. And I will send you books on spirituality to read in the meantime.
Good bye. For now.

GoodByE.

I LEFT THE PRISON GROUNDS AND I FELT I HAD HELPED ONE SOUL.....
DUMM
But WHAT OF THE THOUSANDS MORE that NEEDED HELP. The ALARMING NUMBER OF YOUNG CHILDREN IN PRISON FOR MURDERS WAS STAGGERING. THE PAPERS WERE FULL OF HEADLINES REPORTING CHILDREN MURDERING TEACHERS, MURDERING other CHILDREN, MURDERING family MEMBERS, AND PLANNING SCHOOL BOMBINGS.
GUARD

THE MORE SOPHISTICATED AND COMPLEX THE WORLD BECOMES THE MORE THE VALUES OF LOVE AND KINDNESS ARE DIMINISHED.
NEW MALL COMING SOON!
HELP US PLEESE!
666
U.S.A
I NEED A BEER! HEY, WHY LIE !!!

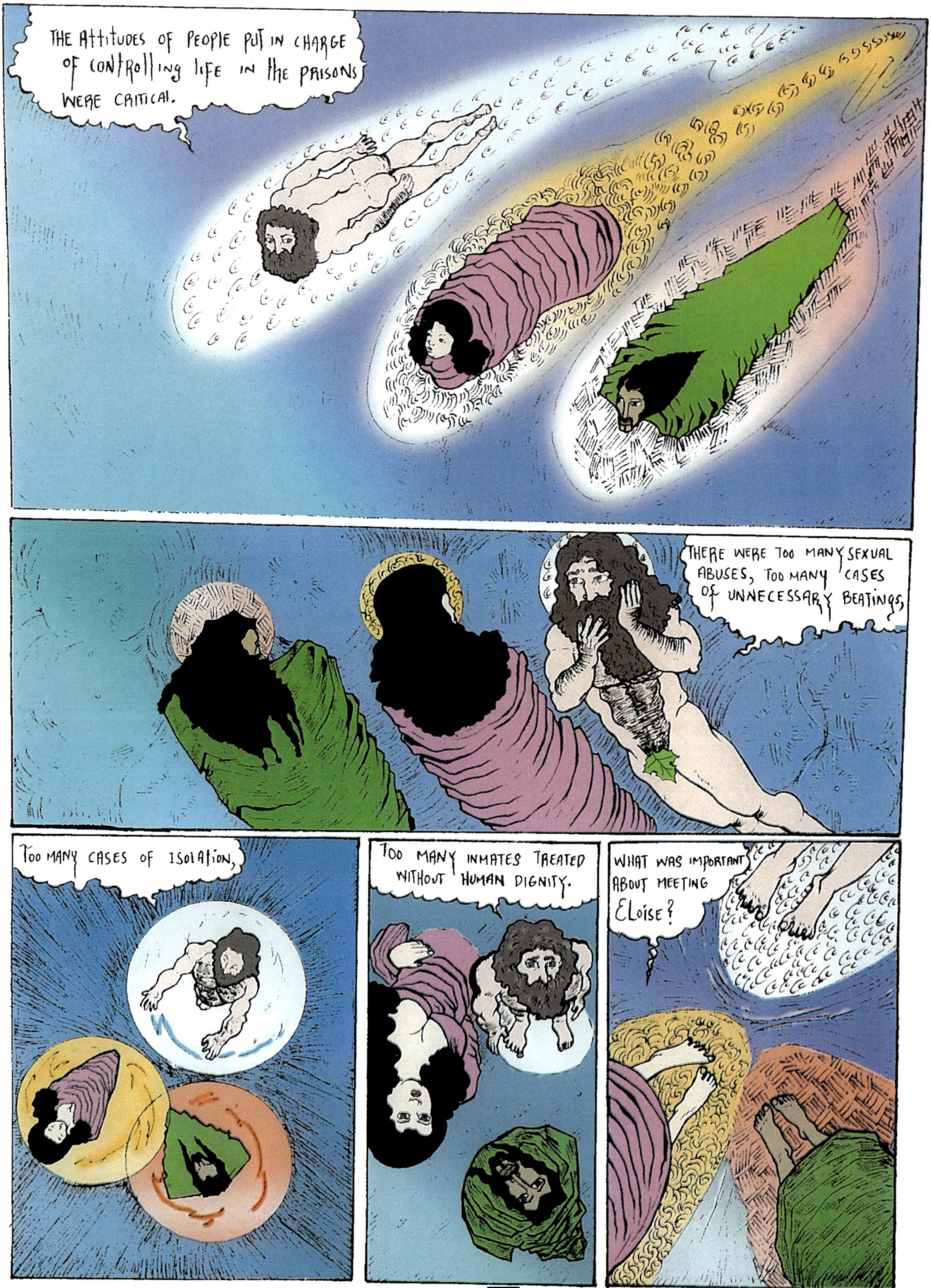

THE Attitudes OF PEOPLE PUT IN CHARGE OF CONTROLLING LIFE IN THE PRISONS WERE CRITICAL.

Some People Have called me a Fool for trying to Change the inadequate System, But I tried to live up to my mission in life and make the world a better Place.
And now that I am gone, I wonder who will take my Place and Bring hope and love to all the other Eloises on the Earth.
You are still giving into your Ego, your image of self - importance. You still want to be lookedup to.
That is not fair Kika.......
You wonder? You wonder?
I chose a challenging occupation.

MY PATIENTS CAME TO ME OUT OF DESPERATION. WHEN THEY COULD NO LONGER TOLERATE THE PAIN OF THEIR LIVES, THEY SOUGHT ME OUT.

THEY DEMANDED THAT I CURE THEIR DIFFICULTIES.
HELP ME... DOC... I'VE... BEEN A RACIST... ALL MY LIFE...!!!

THEY CAME WITH REAL OR IMAGINED ILLNESSES,

WITH FANTASIES, WITH THEIR OWN REALITIES.

SOME CAME BECAUSE THEY POSSESSED AN OBSESSIVE FEAR OF DEATH.

Some came because they were frightened of love, or relationships of life.
Dr. Schmude
They wanted me to play their games, and walk their journey for them. they came to me as if I was their father, and demanded unconditional acceptance from me. I was on the same journey as they were, but they expected answers from me that I did not always have.
Hey... Doc. it seems like you aint got what I wanna hear.
REAL

I GAVE MY PATIENTS HOPE. I PERMITTED THEM TO HAVE THEIR DREAMS.
I GAVE THEM KINDNESS AND LOVE.
You chose the vocation of a Doctor because you wanted to control others. You relished the role of making decisions for the well being of your patients.

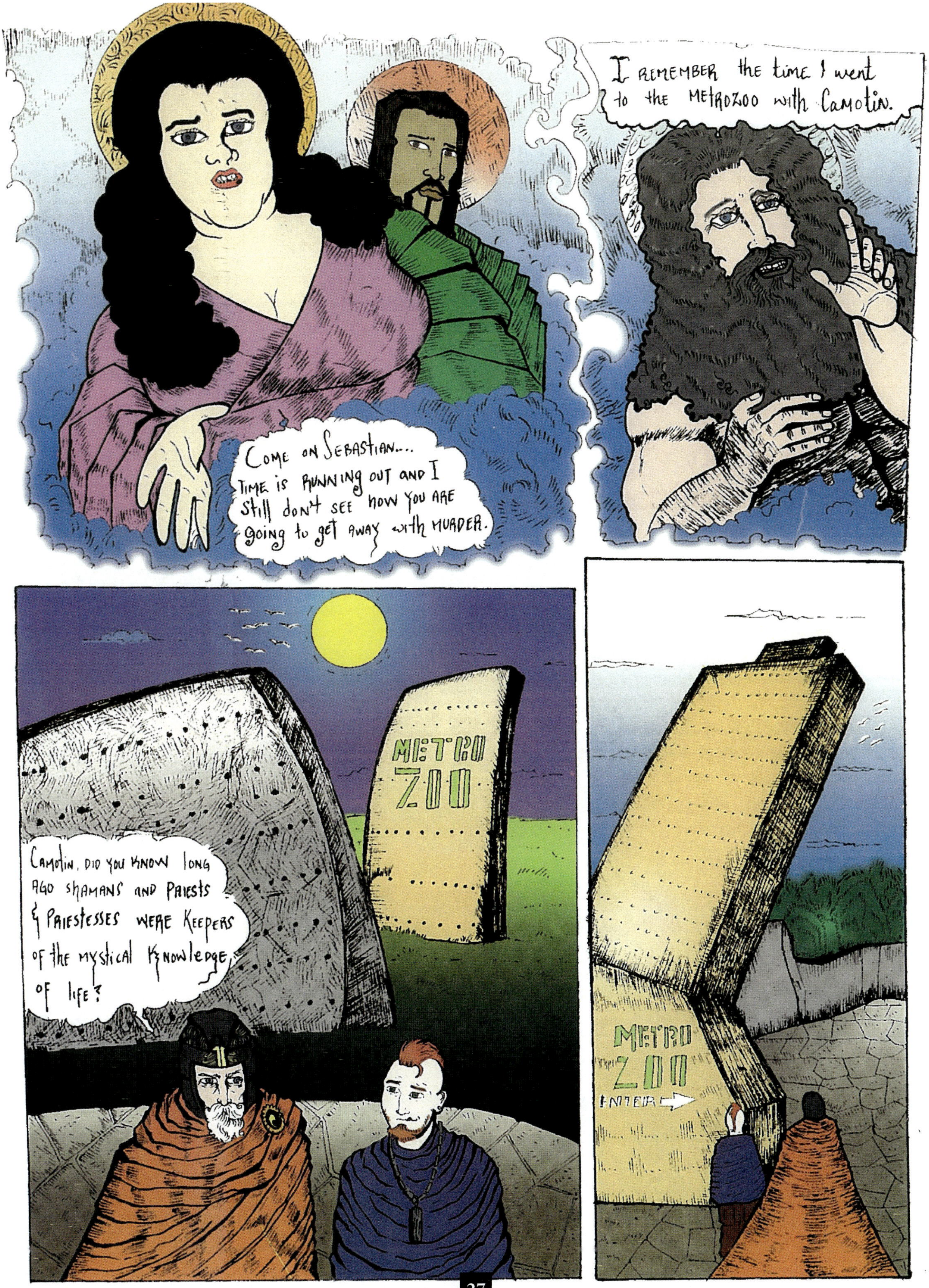

Come on Sebastian... Time is running out and I still don't see how you are going to get away with murder.

I remember the time I went to the Metrozoo with Camotin.

They were tuned into the Language of Nature and the universe. They were the links between the seen and the unseen worlds. They believed all life was sacred, and they knew animals could speak to people who would listen. They would put on animal skins & masks to try and endow themselves with powerful energies.

to awaken natural Rhythms of the Seasons. They were able to bridge the natural world with the supernatural. The laws, which govern the physical and the spiritual world,

cannot be separated. It is said 'as above, so below; as below so above.' All things are connected, and have significance to each other.

There are many dark paradoxes in the secrets of nature, & many obstacles that are hidden from view in the unknown.

oooh... That sounds scary.

METRO ZOO

That is only because you do not understand the significance of knowledge about this subject. Animal imagery is a way to learn about the invisible world and ourselves.
Animals are symbols that represent the emotional side of life, reflecting qualities that we must overcome, control or express differently.
They are symbols of strength associated with the invisible realm that we can manifest in our world. A totem represents each animal.

A TOTEM IS ANY NATURAL OBJECT, BEING OR ANIMAL, WHOSE SPIRIT & ENERGY WE FEEL CLOSELY CONNECTED TO.

There are many stories about a time when there were no boundaries between animals & humans, and they could speak together. It reflected a time between human and divine. Wild and tame had no meaning. The animal world shows us the potentials that are possible. For example, did you know birds represent the symbols of the soul?

Fish, aquatic life and water are the ancient symbols of intuition and the creativity of life. That is why I am so attached to the ocean.

Every area of Nature is woven into our existence.

How come you know so much?

I have studied with many different sages, and shamans. I always want to learn more, because each element of life connects to all others.

Whenever life asks something of us, we should answer with love. Whenever we see conflict, we should respond with harmony.
What!! Man, that shit is hard.

Wherever we see anger, we should respond with calm.
Say Hi! to my ass.... Broker... when you get to Wall Street....., corporate boy... heh! heh! heh!
REBEL
BAD
That was not very nice... sir.

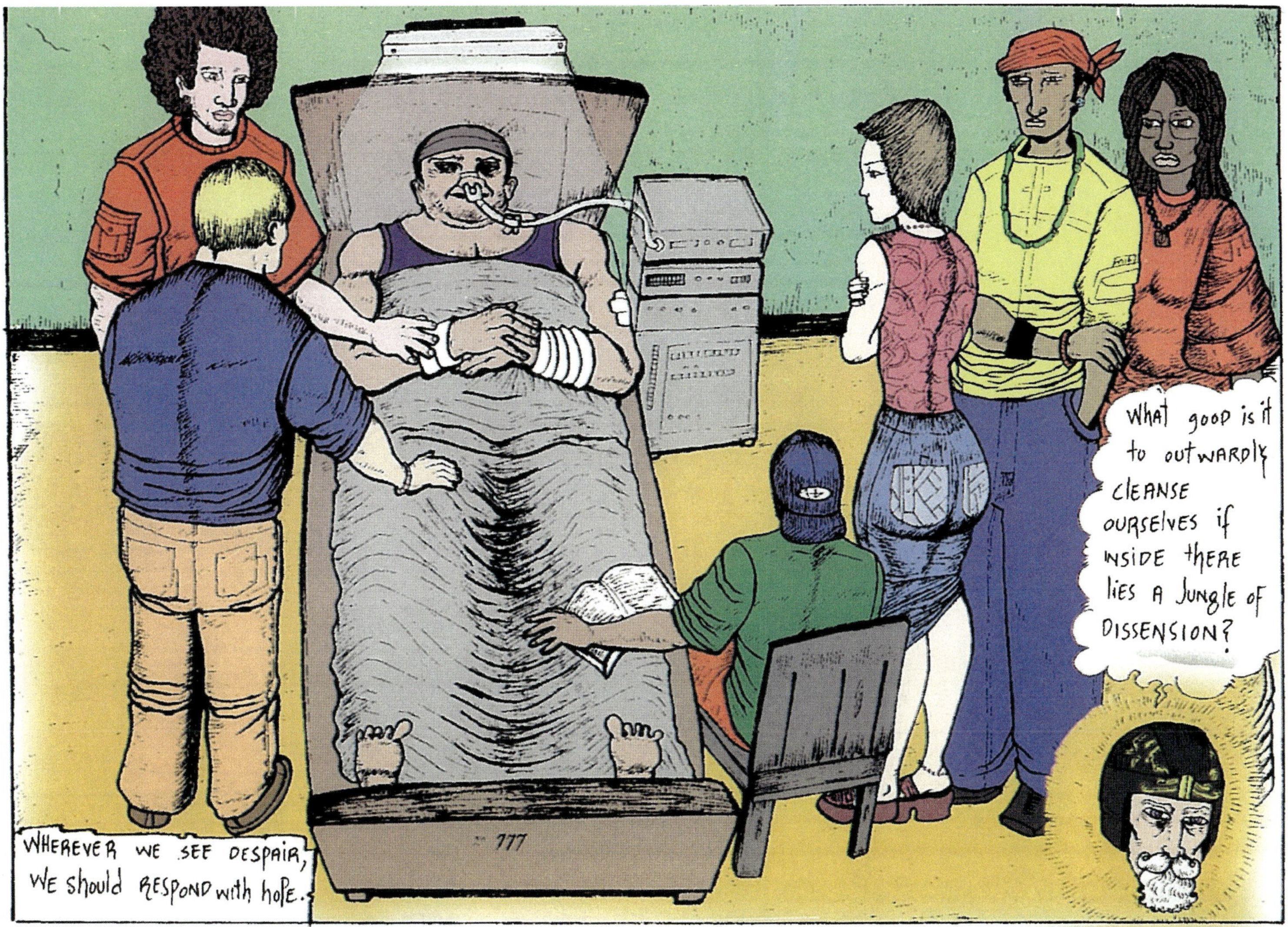

WHEREVER WE SEE DESPAIR, WE should RESPOND with hope.

What good is it to outwardly cleanse ourselves if inside there lies a Jungle of DISSENSION?

I FEEL BADLY FOR THE ANIMALS HERE. THEY Might BE treated well, AND GIVEN FOOD, BUT they ARE NOT FREE.

THEY ARE MANY AMONG US that walk FREE, BUT live AS IF THEY WERE CAGED.

It is our thoughts and closed minds that keep us in prisons.

There are many tragedies and calamities in life.

There are obstacles given to us that are challenges,

To permit us to grow spiritually. When we react instead of being pro-active, we do not accomplish growth.
The light is constantly testing us.

There is much we can gain if we accept our responsibilities, and are willing to make an effort to do the right thing.

What did you learn when you went to the zoo?
Whoever looks for a life that is comfortable and without troubles, will never find it. It is only when we do the right thing, and don't mind being uncomfortable and facing challenges that we will have an easier and better life. It is only through positive change that we can achieve a higher spiritual level, and help our karma for this and future lifetimes.

There were sentences about an angel dressed in a cloud with a rainbow over his head.
His face was like the sun, and his legs like pillars of fire.
He held a little scroll in his hand, and he put his right foot on the sea, and his left foot on the land.

I DECIDED NOT TO DO THE PAST LIFE REGRESSION. INSTEAD I PUT HIM INTO HYPNOSIS. HE SLOWLY WENT TO SLEEP.
MINE
SCRATCH SCRATCH
SCRATCH
HE BEGAN TO TALK ABOUT HIMSELF.
HA HA HA
AND SUDDENLY HE STARTED TALKING ABOUT THE DREAM THAT HE HAD.
It is WINTER, AND I AM cold.
I AM WRAPPED IN A WOOL BLANKET. I AM YOUNG.
I WAKE UP IN THE MIDDLE OF THE NIGHT,
RECALLING A VERY STRANGE DREAM.
THE IMAGES APPEARED TO ME AS ANGELS AND TERRIFYING ANIMALS, FRIGHTENING TO BEHOLD, AND UNLIKE ANYTHING I HAVE EVER SEEN BEFORE.

I was alone,
on a high mountain top. There were no houses visible, nor any people, or animals or even trees or vegetation.

I was holding a book in my hands, and reading from it.

What was the title of the book?
I don't know what the title was.
Do you recall what it was all about?

I remember some of it. I recall the words seven spirits of God, and seven stars.
Poor soul...!

There were sentences about an angel dressed in a cloud with a rainbow over his head.
His face was like the sun, and his legs like pillars of fire.
He held a little scroll in his hand, and he put his right foot on the sea, and his left foot on the land.

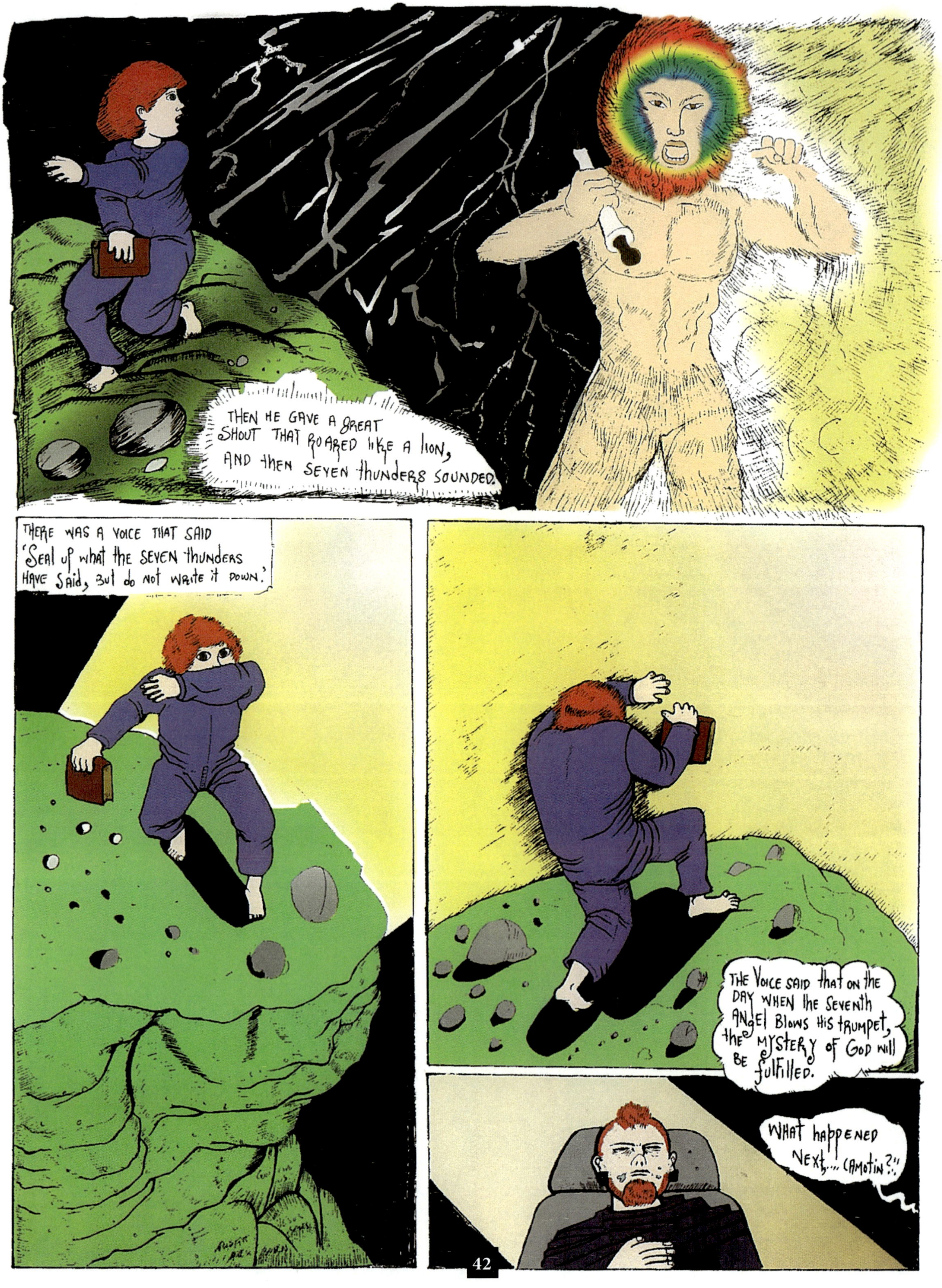

THEN HE GAVE A GREAT SHOUT THAT ROARED LIKE A LION, AND THEN SEVEN THUNDERS SOUNDED.

I SAW A HAND that held A SCROLL WRITTEN ON the INSIDE, AND it WAS SEALED with SEVEN SEALS. Then there WAS A loud voice that ASKED "Who is worthy to open the scroll AND BREAK it's SEALS?" I SAW A LAMB that looked like it HAD BEEN Slaughtered, AND it had SEVEN HORNS AND SEVEN EYES.
All the CREATURES OF HEAVEN AND EARTH, AND UNDER EARTH AND IN THE SEA PRAISED the LAMB, AND WORSHIPPED HIM.
THEN STRANGE THINGS STARTED TO HAPPEN WHEN THE LAMB BEGAN TO OPEN THE SEALS. WHEN HE OPENED THE FIRST ONE A WHITE HORSE APPEARED with A RIDER.

THE RIDER WAS GIVEN A CROWN AND HE CAME OUT AS A CONQUEROR.....
DID HE OPEN THE SECOND SEAL?
YES AND A BRIGHT RED HORSE CAME OUT. HIS RIDER WAS GIVEN A SWORD, AND WAS PERMITTED TO TAKE PEACE FROM THE EARTH.

..So that People would Slaughter One Another.
POW

When the third seal was opened a black horse appeared. His rider held a pair of scales in his hand.
A voice told him something about not damaging the olive oil and wine as he worked.
It was something about wheat and barley for a day's pay.
What happened next?
Many things are vague. I am surprised I can remember this much. I will try to go on. The fourth seal was broken and a pale green horse appeared.

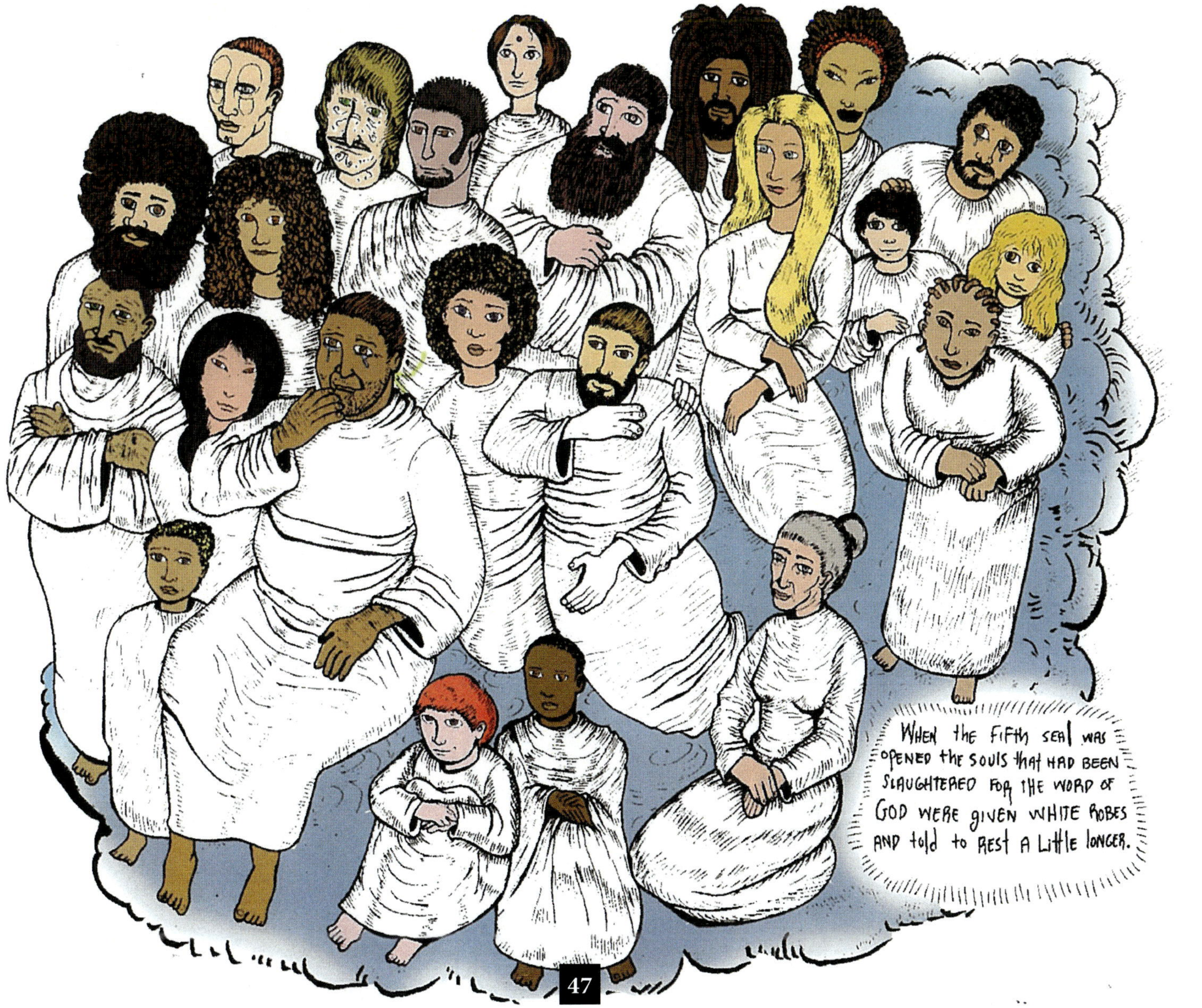

WHEN THE FIFTH SEAL WAS OPENED THE SOULS THAT HAD BEEN SLAUGHTERED FOR THE WORD OF GOD WERE GIVEN WHITE ROBES AND TOLD TO REST A LITTLE LONGER.

When the sixth seal was opened there was a great earthquake, and the sun became black,
STOP
And the full moon became blood red.
The stars fell to the Earth,
And the sky vanished.

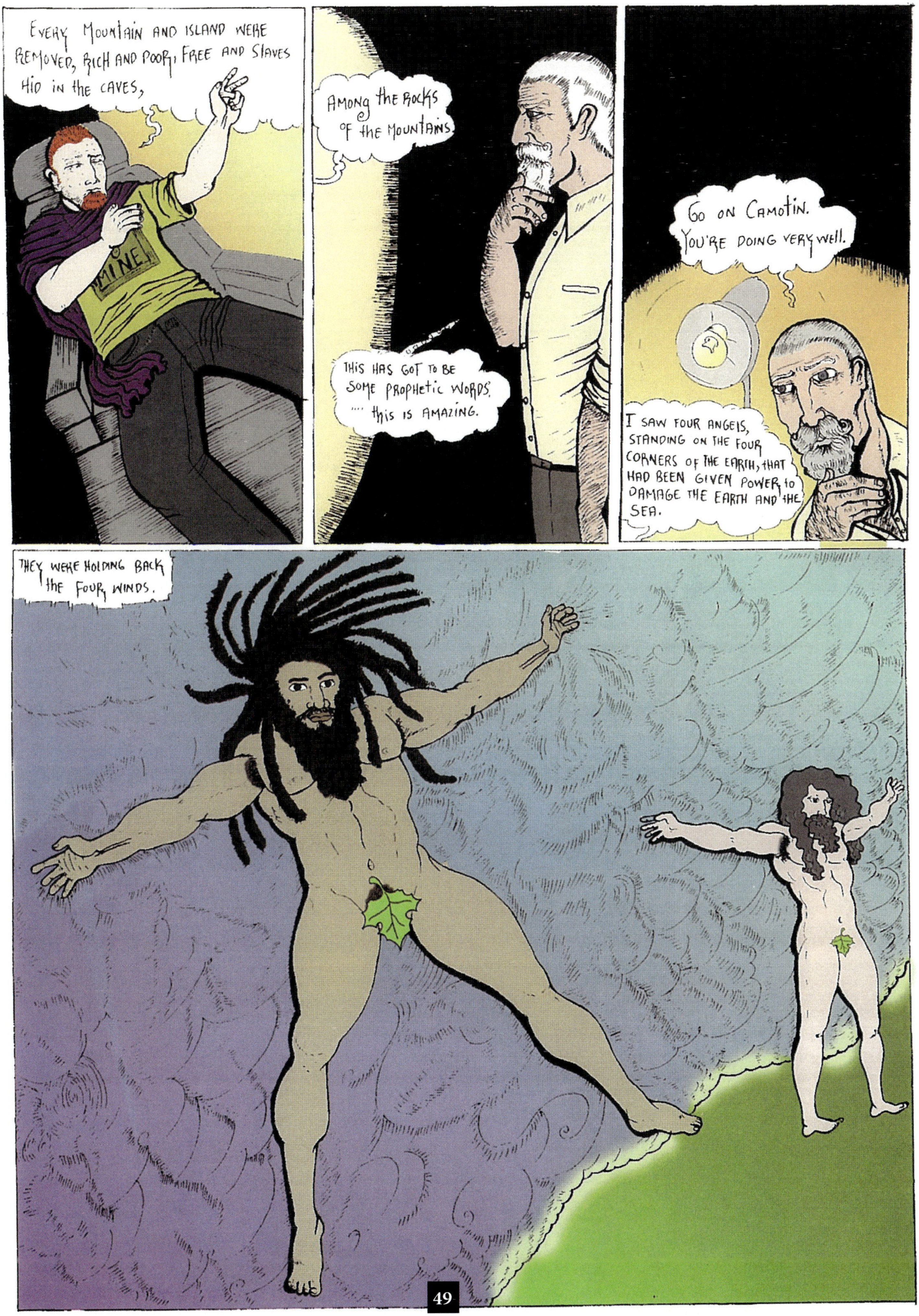

They were holding back the four winds.

There was another angel holding the SEAL of GOD, AND he said that there was to Be No damage Done until the SERVANTS of God had A SEAl placed on their foreheads.

One Hundred fourty four thousand from Every Tribe from the people in Israel were sealed.
Then there appeared multitudes of people, too numerous to count, from every nation and tribe, people who spoke many languages.

Some one asked who they were,
...And an angel answered they have come out of a great ordeal, and now their garments are white.
The angel said the one who was seated on the throne would shelter them, and they would hunger and thirst...
...No more, and neither the sun or scorching heat would strike them.

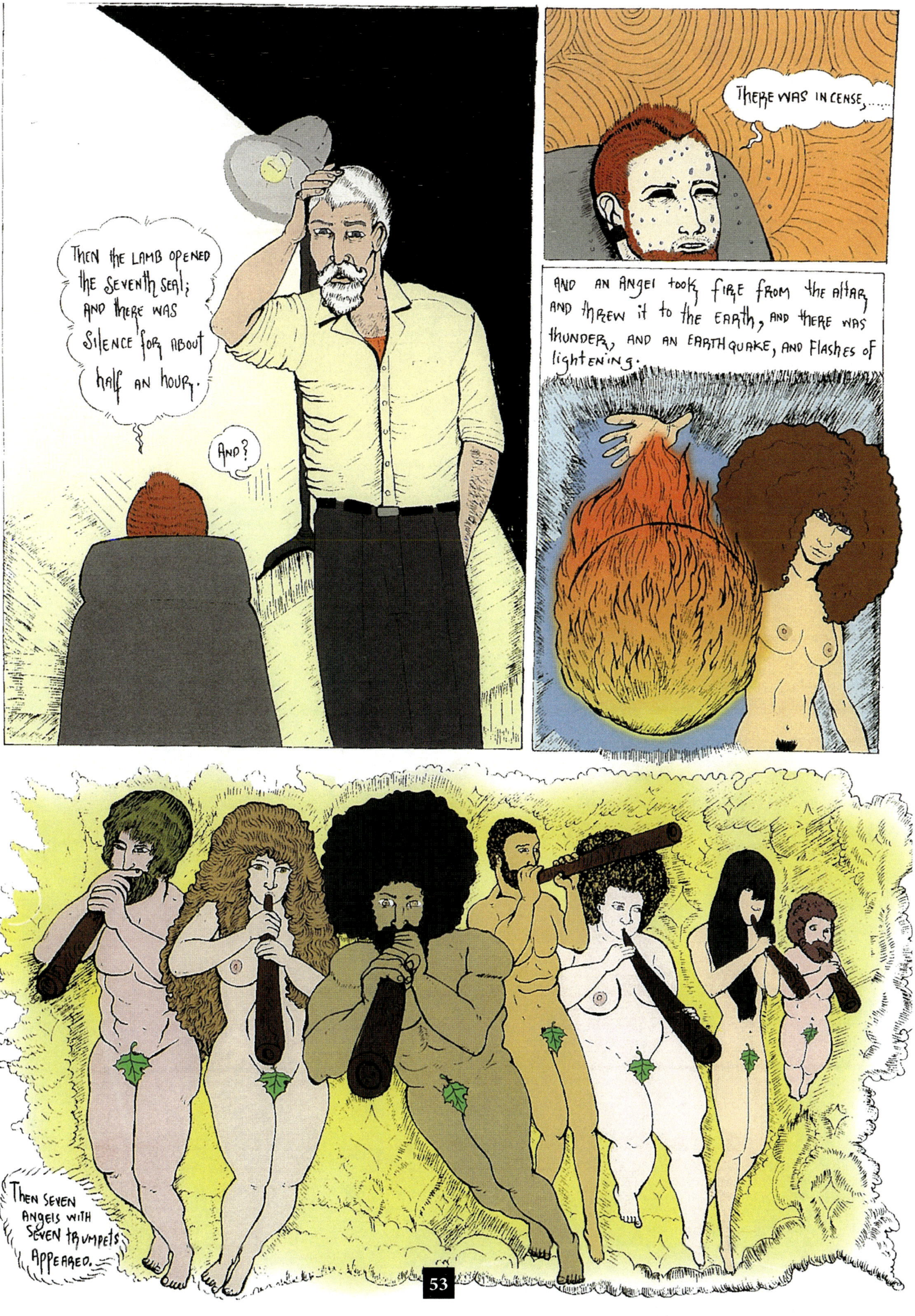

Then the lamb opened the seventh seal; and there was silence for about half an hour.

And?

And an angel took fire from the altar and threw it to the earth, and there was thunder, and an earthquake, and flashes of lightening.

Then seven angels with seven trumpets appeared.

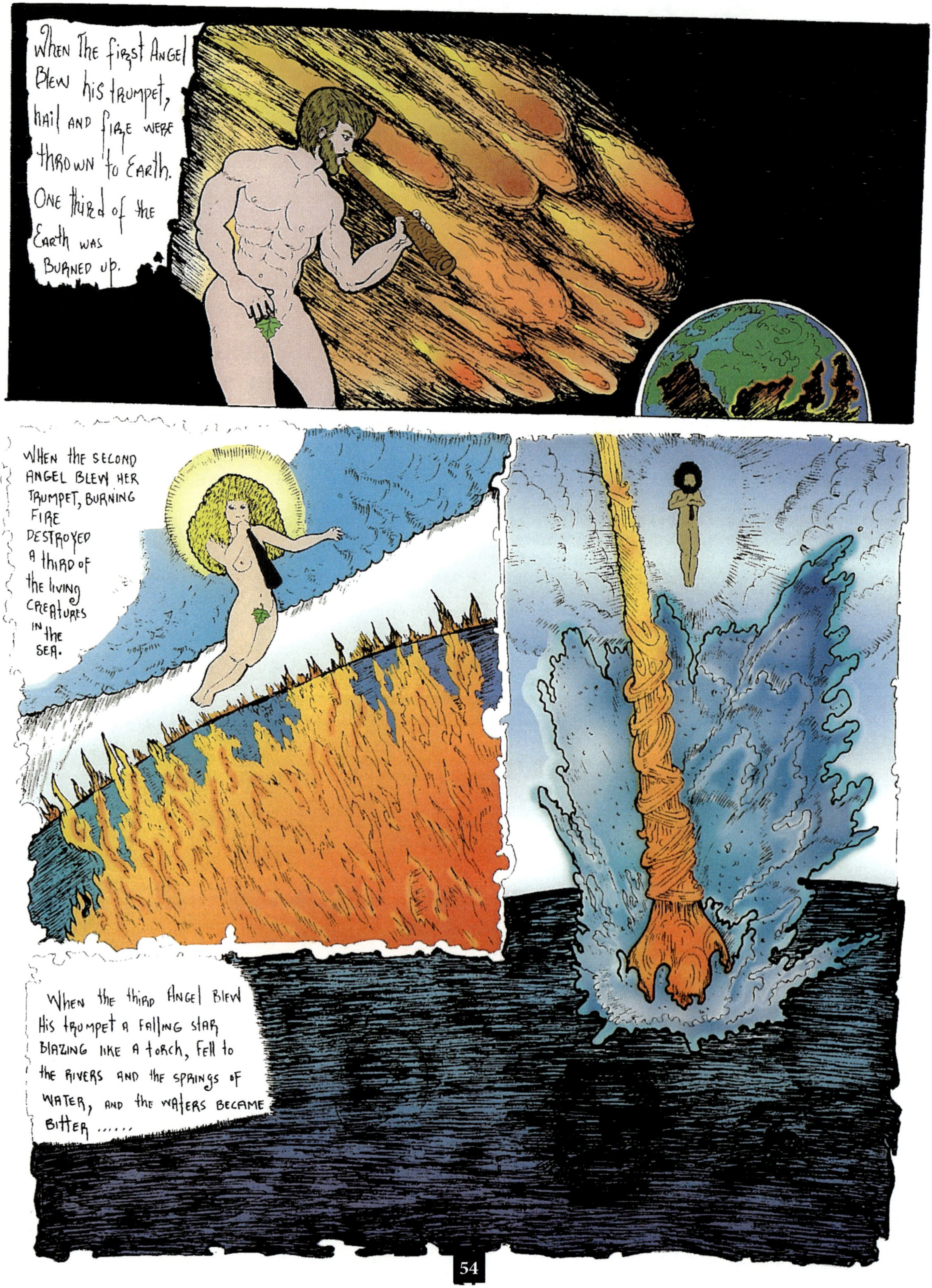

When the second Angel blew her trumpet, burning fire destroyed a third of the living creatures in the sea.

When the third Angel Blew His trumpet a falling star blazing like a torch, fell to the rivers and the springs of water, and the waters became bitter ......

...And Caused Death to many who drank from it.
WATER
2030
Then the Fourth Angel blew his trumpet......
... AND A THIRD OF THE SUN, AND A third of the MOON, AND A third of the stars were struck. A third of the DAY was kept FROM shining AND ALSO the moon.

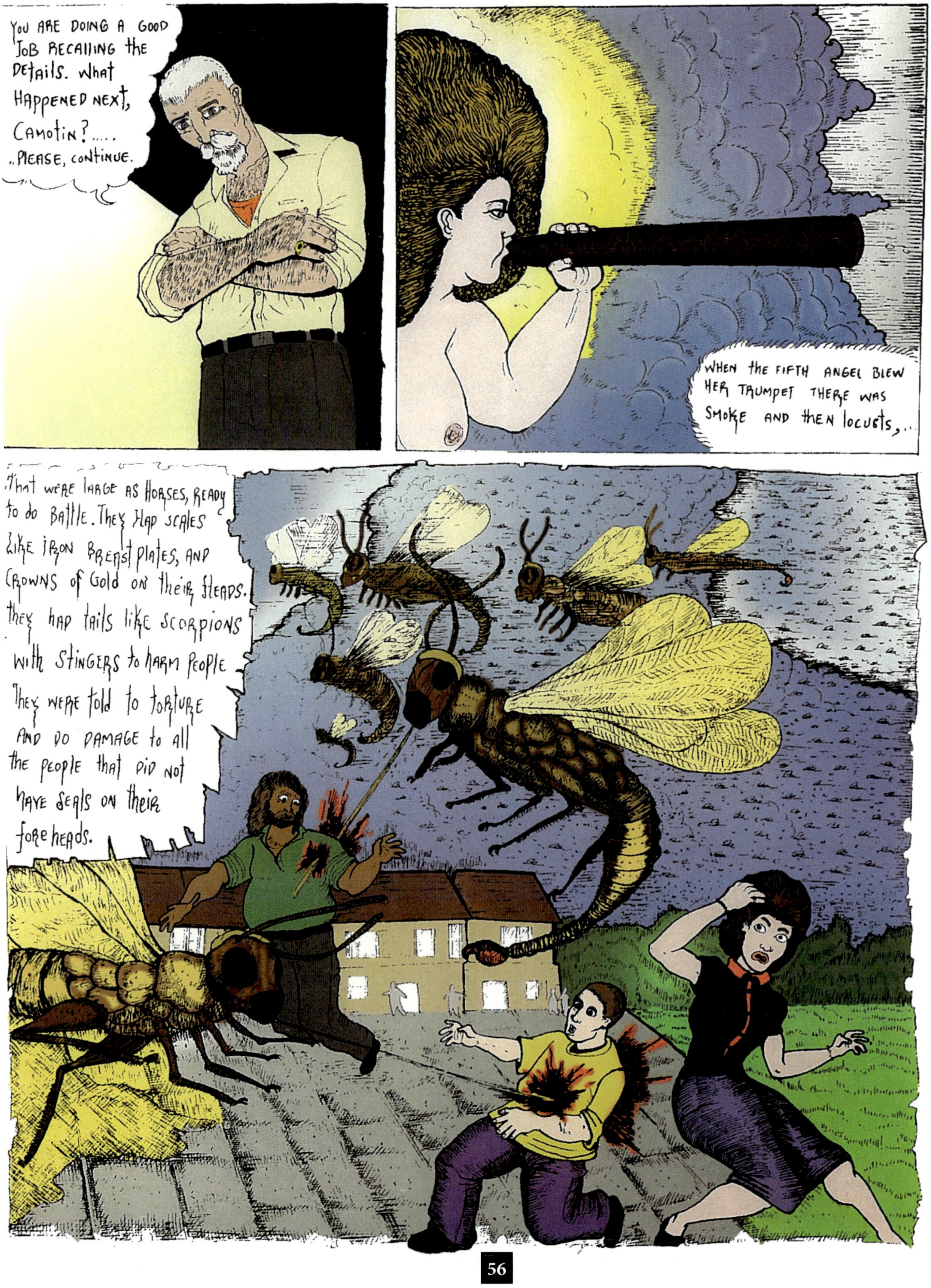

That were large as horses, ready to do battle. They had scales like iron breast plates, and crowns of gold on their heads. They had tails like scorpions with stingers to harm people They were told to torture and do damage to all the people that did not have seals on their fore heads.

THEN the sixth ANGEL BLEW HER trumpet, AND FOUR ANGELS WHO HAD BEEN HELD PRISONERS... WERE.......

..RELEASED SO THEY COULD KILL ONE third OF HUMANKIND.

THERE WERE HORSES with HEADS like lions, AND FIRE AND SMOKE CAME FROM their mouths.
then the Seventh ANGEl BLEW His trumpet AND God's temple in HEAVEN WAS OPENED, AND there was A BIG thunder.
AND Rumblings, AND flashes of lightning,

WOW!
...AND AN EARTHQUAKE.... AND HEAVY FIRE. THEN I SAW A PREGNANT WOMAN CRYING OUT IN THE PAIN OF CHILD BIRTH,....

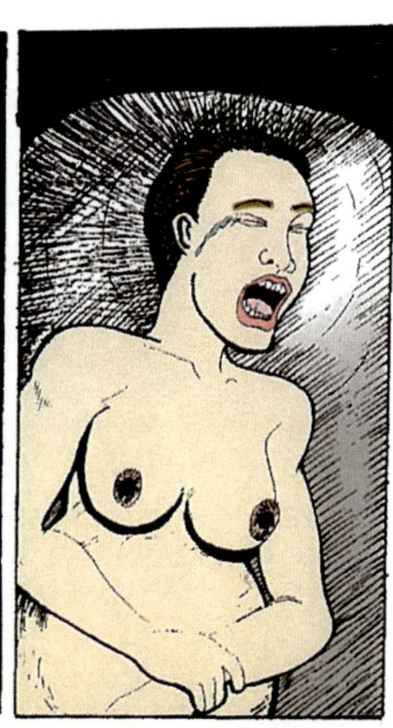

..AND THERE WAS A GREAT RED DRAGON WITH SEVEN HEADS THAT WANTED TO DEVOUR HER CHILD WHEN IT WAS BORN. WHEN SHE GAVE BIRTH TO A SON WHO WAS SUPPOSED TO RULE THE EARTH,.....

THE BABY WAS TAKEN FROM HER AND BROUGHT TO GOD. A WAR BROKE OUT IN HEAVEN.

THERE WAS A FIGHT, AND THE DRAGON AND HIS ANGELS WERE DEFEATED.
THEY WERE NOT ALLOWED TO REMAIN IN HEAVEN, AND THE DRAGON AND HIS EVIL ANGELS WERE THROWN DOWN TO EARTH.
WHAT HAPPENED TO THOSE WHO WORSHIPPED THE DRAGON ?!!

THEY WERE TORMENTED.
ROOM FOR RENT ONLY
CODED CITIZEN & RESIDENTS WITH
CODES
NEXT LEVEL NEWS!
NO JOBS....
DON'T BE LOST!!

THERE WAS A CALL FROM HEAVEN FOR THE SAINTS TO KEEP GOD'S COMMANDMENTS AND TO HAVE ENDURANCE.

THEN THE SEVEN ANGELS CAME BEARING THE SEVEN PLAGUES.
THEY POURED THE SEVEN WRATHS OF GOD, FROM SEVEN GOLDEN BOWLS. THERE WAS DEATH AND DESTRUCTION EVERY WHERE.

THEN THE HEAVENS OPENED AND A WHITE HORSE APPEARED.
HIS RIDER WAS CALLED FAITHFUL AND TRUE.
AN ANGEL CAME DOWN FROM HEAVEN, AND FOUND THE DRAGON.

HE BOUND HIM AND threw him INTO A BOTTOMLESS Pit which WAS locked AND SEALED.
WHAT happened to this DRAGON?
HE WAS told he would REMAIN there FOR ONE thousAND YEARS, so that HE WOULD not DECEIVE the NATIONS ANYMORE, AND then HE would BE let out FOR A short while.

Then I saw a new heaven and a new earth, and I heard an angel say that God will dwell among mortals, and Death will be no more, and mourning and crying and pain will be no more.
Then I woke up from my dream, but everything seemed so real.
Ahhh..... I see; that's truly amazing.
I don't quite understand what it meant.
You have dreamed about the Revelation, and John and the portion about the Apocalypses.
You must have read that part of the Bible at some time in your life.
I have never read the Bible Doctor.

THERE HAVE BEEN MANY VERSIONS OF PORTIONS OF THE BIBLE, DEPENDING ON WHO WROTE THEM.
THERE ARE MANY..... DIFFERENCES. THERE IS MUCH CONFUSION ABOUT THE MESSAGES THAT ARE GIVEN.
ORIGINALLY, IDEAS WERE NEVER WRITTEN DOWN, AND STORIES WERE TOLD VERBALLY. WHEN THINGS ARE PASSED DOWN THAT MANY TIMES THERE ARE BOUND TO BE DIFFERENCES IN THE TELLING, AND THE INTERPRETATIONS. SOME PEOPLE CLAIM THE STORIES HAVE NO TRUTH, AND ARE MYTHS. OTHERS BELIEVE THEM TO BE TRUE.

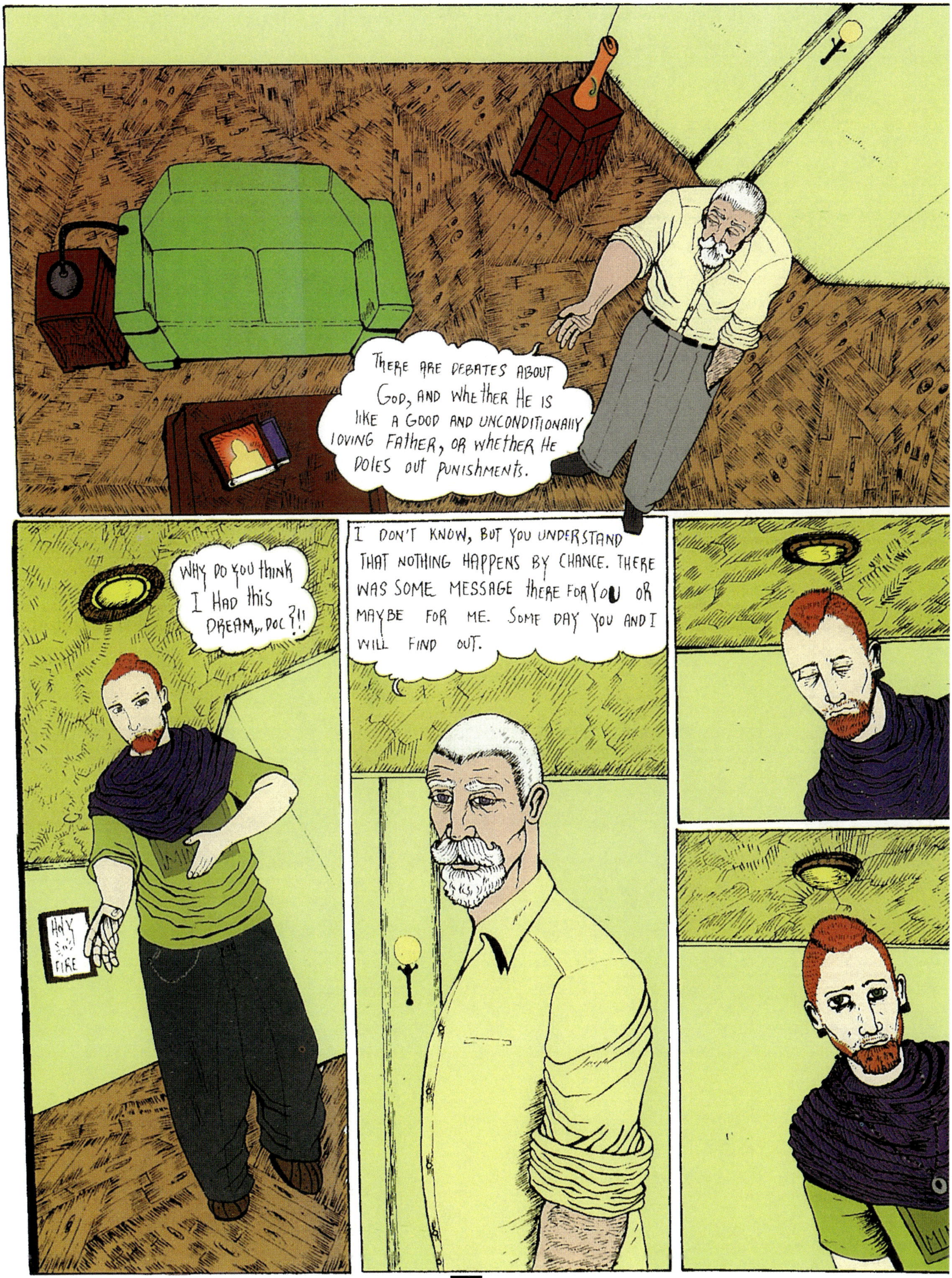

THERE ARE DEBATES ABOUT GOD, AND WHETHER HE IS LIKE A GOOD AND UNCONDITIONALLY LOVING FATHER, OR WHETHER HE DOLES OUT PUNISHMENTS.

Do you recall any moment in your life or meeting any person who brought you a message that you did not want to hear.

HE WAS A CATHOLIC PRIEST.
I VISITED HIM IN A PSYCHIATRIC HOSPITAL.
GLORY BE.... COME DOWN TO PLAY... GLORY BE ....YES, OH, YES!
HEY, ORDERLY
FATHER O'BRIAN WAS ACCUSED OF TRYING TO KILL A YOUNG ARAB MAN WHO HE BELIEVED WAS IN SOME WAY CONNECTED TO THE ANTI-CHRIST.
NUTCASE ROOM № 7
THE CHURCH DID NOT WANT WORD OF THIS MURDER ATTEMPT TO REACH THE NEWSPAPERS BECAUSE IT MIGHT POSE TO BE AN EMBARRASSMENT, RAISE MANY QUESTIONS AND COULD BECOME A TROUBLESOME ISSUE.
FATHER O'BRIAN WAS CONSIDERED A "PROPHET" IN CERTAIN CHRISTIAN CONSERVATIVES CIRCLES

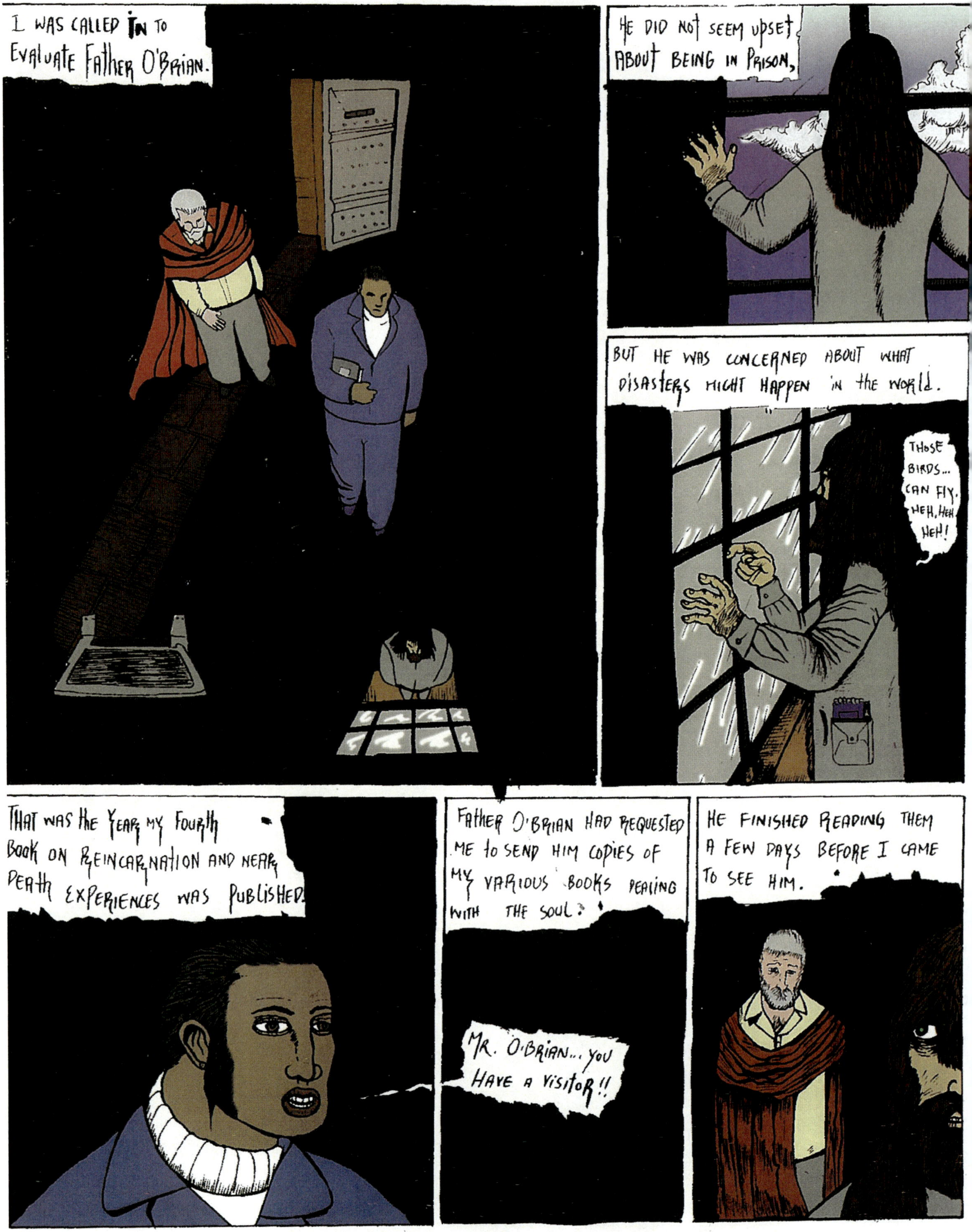

I WAS CALLED IN TO EVALUATE FATHER O'BRIAN.

He made a list of comments and he partially agreed with some of my philosophies.

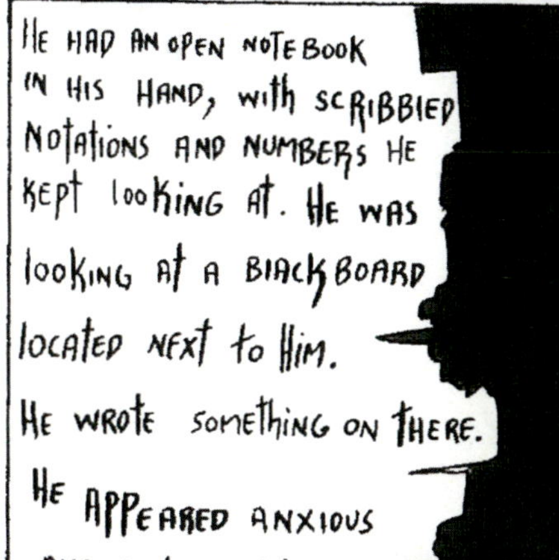
He had an open notebook in his hand, with scribbled notations and numbers he kept looking at. He was looking at a blackboard located next to him.
He wrote something on there.
He appeared anxious and distraught.

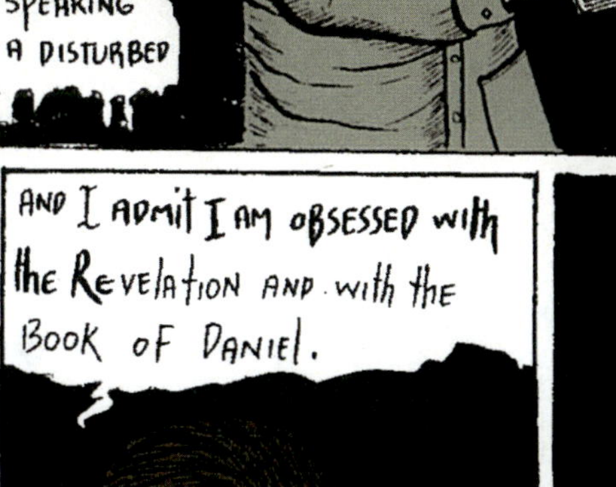
He began speaking to me in a disturbed manner.
Dr. Camote are you familiar with the Bible?
Yes. I am..... indeed!!!

I have studied the Old and the New Testament in depth,

and I admit I am obsessed with the Revelation and with the Book of Daniel.

Are you aware that the Apocalypses and the Book of Daniel always refer to the number seven?

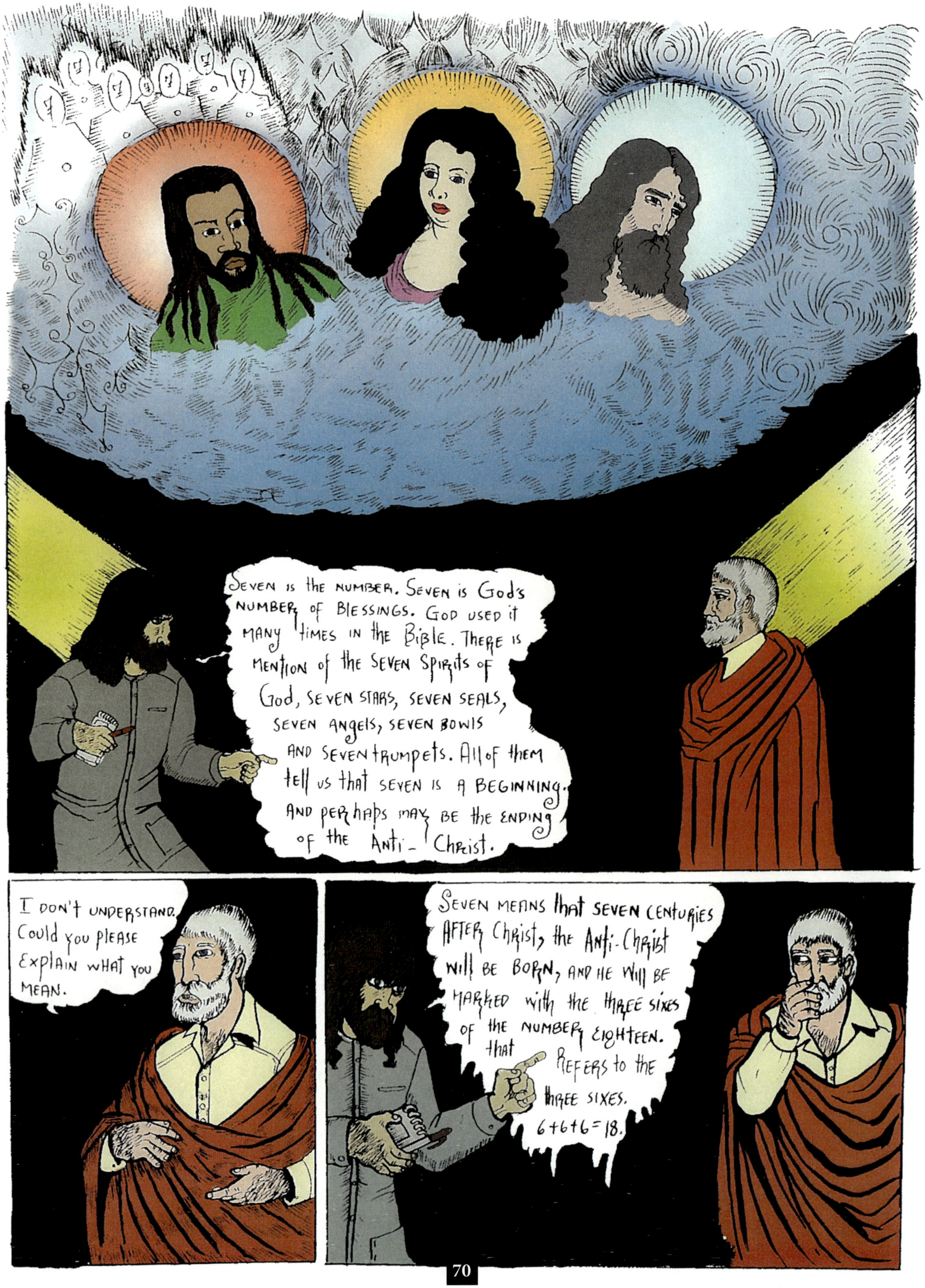

Seven is the number. Seven is God's number of blessings. God used it many times in the Bible. There is mention of the seven Spirits of God, seven stars, seven seals, seven angels, seven bowls and seven trumpets. All of them tell us that seven is a beginning. And perhaps may be the ending of the Anti-Christ.

IN THE BIBLE NUMBER 18 IS A CODE. THAT CODE CAN BE ALSO INTERPRETED IN MANY WAYS.
WE HAVE TO CLOSELY EXAMINE EVERY SITUATION IN ORDER TO FIND THE NUMBER 18.
I BELIEVE ONE OF THE SIGNS OF THE NUMBER 18 WILL BE THE NUMBER OF LETTERS THAT WILL COMPOSE THE NAME OF THE ANTI-CHRIST.
THROUGH DIFFERENT TIMES AND PERIODS, SOME SCHOLARS HAVE CHOSEN CENTURIES, OTHERS HAVE CHOSEN NUMBERS OR YEARS TO TRY TO FIND THE NUMBER OR THE CODE.
BE OPEN MINDED.
I HAVE REACHED A CONCLUSION ABOUT THAT NAME AND THE CODE.
I WOULD LOVE TO KNOW THE NAME AND THE CODE MYSELF.
WHEN I WAS YOUNGER I SPENT SOME TIME IN AN ANCIENT SPANISH MONASTERY AND I HAD THE OPPORTUNITY TO SEE SOME VERY OLD MANUSCRIPTS DATING BACK TO THE EIGHTH CENTURY.

I'm listening to you Father, but that is an old theory that some Christian writers and politicians believed in the Middle Ages. In the eighth century in Spain a manuscript was found falsely stating that Mohammed died in the year 666, making him the Anti-Christ. That was long ago when Christians were fighting the Muslim expansion through Europe and later on during the Crusades.

listen to me. the Revelation says "let anyone with understanding calculate the number of the Beast." Christ died in the year 34 of the Christian era when he was 33 years old. Mohammed died in the year 632 of the Christian era. If you add the dates you will get 632+34=666. The year of the Death of Christ plus the year of the Death of the Anti-Christ will be the year 666. That will be the fulfillment of the code. The number 666 can also be calculated in another way.

THE Muslims started the Holy WAR following the Death of the Prophet in the Year 633.
THE AGE OF CHRIST WHEN HE DIED WAS 33. ADDING the NUMBERS AGAIN WE GET 633+33= 666 OR 6+3+3+3+3=18.
Either way it still configures 666 or the number of the Anti-Christ,
But I BELIEVE the 632+34 that is 6+3+2+3+4=18 is the REAL ONE.
Still Father. THOSE NUMBERS CAN BE JUST A COINCIDENCE.
I thought YOU DIDN'T BELIEVE IN COINCIDENCES DR.
Not REALLY Father But.........

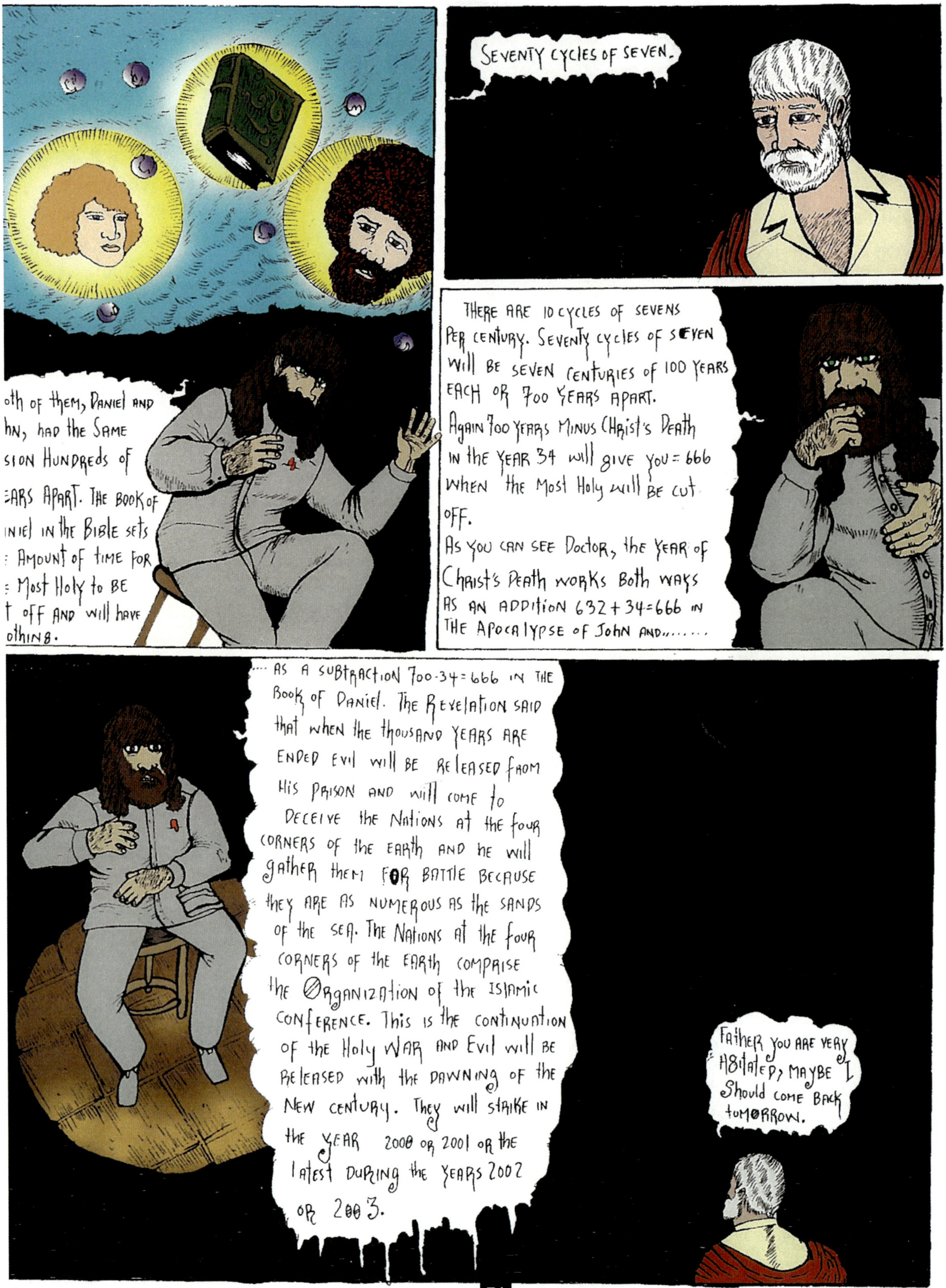

There are 10 cycles of sevens per century. Seventy cycles of seven will be seven centuries of 100 years each or 700 years apart.
Again 700 years minus Christ's Death in the year 34 will give you = 666 when the Most Holy will be cut off.
As you can see Doctor, the year of Christ's Death works both ways as an addition 632 + 34 = 666 in the Apocalypse of John and.......

.... as a subtraction 700 - 34 = 666 in the Book of Daniel. The Revelation said that when the thousand years are ended Evil will be released from his prison and will come to deceive the Nations at the four corners of the earth and he will gather them for battle because they are as numerous as the sands of the sea. The Nations at the four corners of the earth comprise the Organization of the Islamic Conference. This is the continuation of the Holy War and Evil will be released with the dawning of the new century. They will strike in the year 2000 or 2001 or the latest during the years 2002 or 2003.

Father you are very agitated, maybe I should come back tomorrow.

I believe, Dr. Camote, that the one thousand years the Revelation talks about are not necessarily exact, but in some cases they are pretty close.
Mohammed was born on August 29th, 570.
Again, 570 is the six century first six, and 5+7+0= 12. Again we have the number 18. Anyway, one thousand years later in 1571, the Muslims suffered a tremendous defeat at Lepanto that contained their expansion, but was not as Europe hoped,
the beginning of the disintegration of Islam.
Lepanto?
After Lepanto, radical Muslims went into a lethargic state. And now on the verge of the twenty-first century leaders of Radical Islamic terrorism are looking for a united Muslim World under a common political structure, a global dictatorship like a modern version of the caliphate that provided an early form of Islamic government after the death of the Prophet in the seventh century.
Their final goal is to unite all Muslims of the world and establish a government that follows the rule of the caliphs.

Do you understand?
No, I don't understand, But I am listening to you.
Seven is the number. Seven centuries later in the fourteenth century, the Islamic Ottoman Empire was born to continue the struggle to conquer the world.
One century later they destroyed the Byzantine Empire.
Seven centuries of war ended with a Muslim victory. We will most likely see the next evil attack of Islam in the next century, the twenty-first century, another seven centuries later.
It will be in the twenty-first century when they will finally try to terminate all of us.
They will try to overthrow all Muslim governments that disagree with their views and eventually they will attempt to take over the Western world and make us live in a whole world dominated by their view of Islam and under the law of Allah.

Christians and Muslims Have Had many problems and their wars Have been going on for Centuries, but that does not necessarily mean anything.
THE Anti-Christ is against the Christ Believers and Islam and Christianity Have been battling since the year 623 Just after the Hegira.

Dr. Camote you Have to understand the meaning of the six numbers. The seventh century is the year of the six because everthing is a six, and we have the year 666. In the year 666 the Muslims already completed their first part of the conquest and the expansion of the W O R L D.

By 666 Islam Already Had the Whole Arabian Peninsula, Palestine and Syria, Egypt and Libya, Mesopotamia, Armenia and Persia.

Mohammed was orphaned at six. In the year 630 Mohammed and his men marched into Mecca. Two years later in the sixth day of the sixth month of the year 632 Mohammed died when he was sixty-two.

What you said does Prove Anythin Muslims Believe Christ one of greatest Prophets they Respe And Admire

Well!!
YOU ARE MISSING MY POINT, Doctor.
THEY BELIEVE IN Christ AS A Prophet AND AT THE SAME TIME, THEY TAKE AWAY THE Divinity of Christ.
Father if you ARE NOT A Christian You Don't have to Believe in the Divinity of Christ. They Dont Believe in the Divinity of Mohammed either.

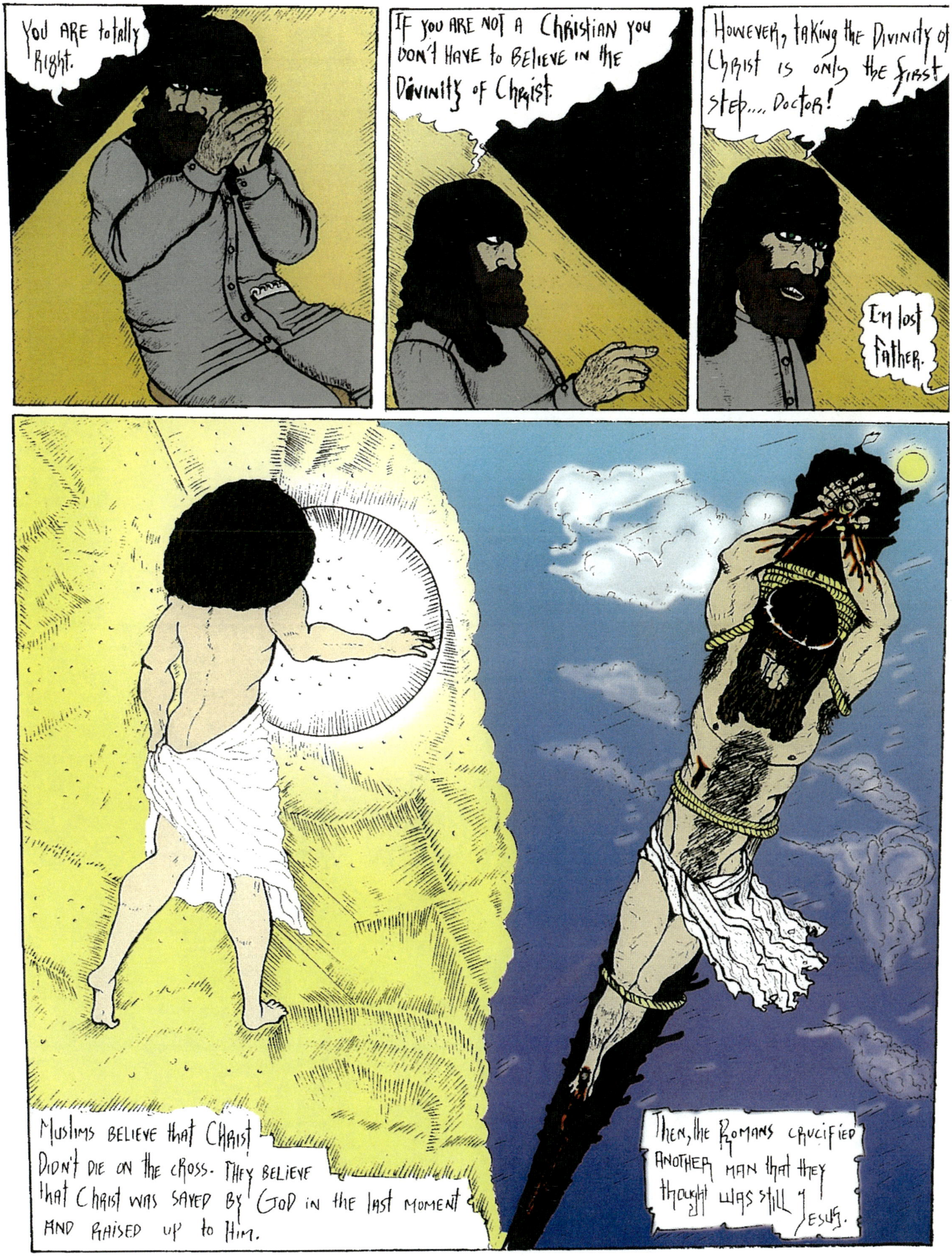

Muslims believe that Christ didn't die on the cross. They believe that Christ was saved by God in the last moment and raised up to Him.

Then, the Romans crucified another man that they thought was still Jesus.

Without this Belief we are left with nothing .... this is the end of our belief. This is the anti-Christ, the end of Christ's great message.

They subtly destroy our Beliefs. Our Belief in the Trinity, the Father, the Son and the Holy Ghost is destroyed.

They affirm in the Koran against the Belief in the Trinity Because they say there is no God But one God and a painful punishment will befall on the DisBelievers.

Muslims believe that the Doctrine of the Holy Trinity is polytheistic. They reject a God incarnation in any form of Human Being or any form of God.
Some Muslim scholars believe that we deleted from the Bible the prophecy of the coming of Mohammed.

I'm not familiar with that part Father.

They Believe that Jesus said: "I am the apostle of God sent to you and I'm bringing you the Good News of an Illustrious Apostle who shall come after me and whose name shall be "Ahmed".

Father there are no original documents upon which Christianity is founded.
Any point under dispute will remain a source of controversy.
Why will they go so far in destroying all our beliefs? Do you know any religion that destroys the beliefs of any other religion in order to overcome it?
But Father.....
The Book of Daniel says that the Beast will speak against the Most High. For us Christians the Most High is no other than Jesus. The Book continues "He will oppress the Saints and will try to change the set times and the Law." In 623 they changed the set times as the Book of Daniel said.

The Islamic calendar is made up of twelve lunar months alternating twenty-nine and 30 days. The Muslim calendar is 354 days long. It is 11 days shorter than our Gregorian solar calendar. The Muslim months do not indicate the season, as they commence earlier by eleven days every year.
Then, they change the law. The law of them is the law of God established in the Koran. But there's more.
Oh, man!

"In 628 Mohammed Defeated the Jews of Khaybar. They became vassals of Medina. That was the Beginning of the Reign of the Anti-Christ.
In January 629 Mohammed took total authority over His Domain.

He started the preparation to lead the lesser Pilgrimage to the Kaaba. When Mohammed and his Followers approached The Sanctuary in the City of Mecca, the Enemies of Mohammed left the city.

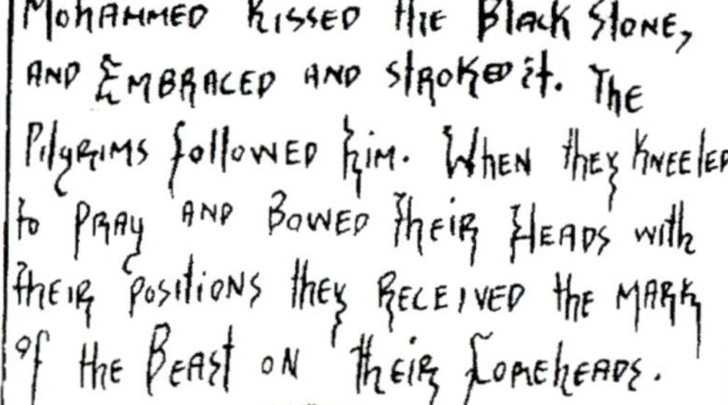
Mohammed kissed the Black Stone, and Embraced and stroked it. The Pilgrims followed him. When they kneeled to pray and bowed their heads with their positions they received the mark of the Beast on their foreheads.

The Revelation said 'Small & Great, Both Rich and Poor, Both Free and Slave, to be marked on the Right hand or the foreHead with the Name of the Beast or the number of its name'.

This Period of total Power lasted Forty-two Months.
What Does this Forty-two Months mean to you?
The Revelation said the beast was allowed to exercise authority for forty-two months. Also it was allowed to make war on the saints and to conquer them. A few months later Mohammed conquered Mecca. A few months later the Christian King of Israel and all of the Jewish settlements paid tribute to him.

That was the preparation of the Holy War and the 42 Months of Power of the Anti-Christ. Christians and Jews became Vassals of Mohammed in the Holy Land. The Revelation said "And every Island fled away, and no mountains were to be found." No Islands, No Mountains, just the Desert, Doctor the Arabian Desert. Do you remember what the Angel of God said to Hagar?
Father, Right Now I do not recall who Hagar is in the Bible.
Hagar was the Egyptian Slave of Abraham. She had Abraham's First son.
Well, I remember now but I don't exactly remember what the Angel of God told her.

The Angel said "I will grant you many descendants. They will be so many that they will be uncountable. You are pregnant and will give birth to a son. You must name him Ishmael.'

I KNOW THAT, FATHER.

THE ARABS CONSIDER THEMSELVES TO BE DIRECT DESCENDANTS OF ISHMAEL.
I'M CRAZY
HUG ME PLEASE
OH! YES!

THEN THE ANGEL CONTINUED....

"HE WILL BE A REBEL. HIS HAND WILL BE AGAINST EVERYONE AND EVERYONE'S HAND WILL BE AGAINST HIM. STILL HE WILL DWELL UNDISTURBED NEAR ALL HIS BROTHERS."
ISHMAEL HAD TWELVE SONS AND THEY BECAME PRINCES OF THE ARAB N NS.

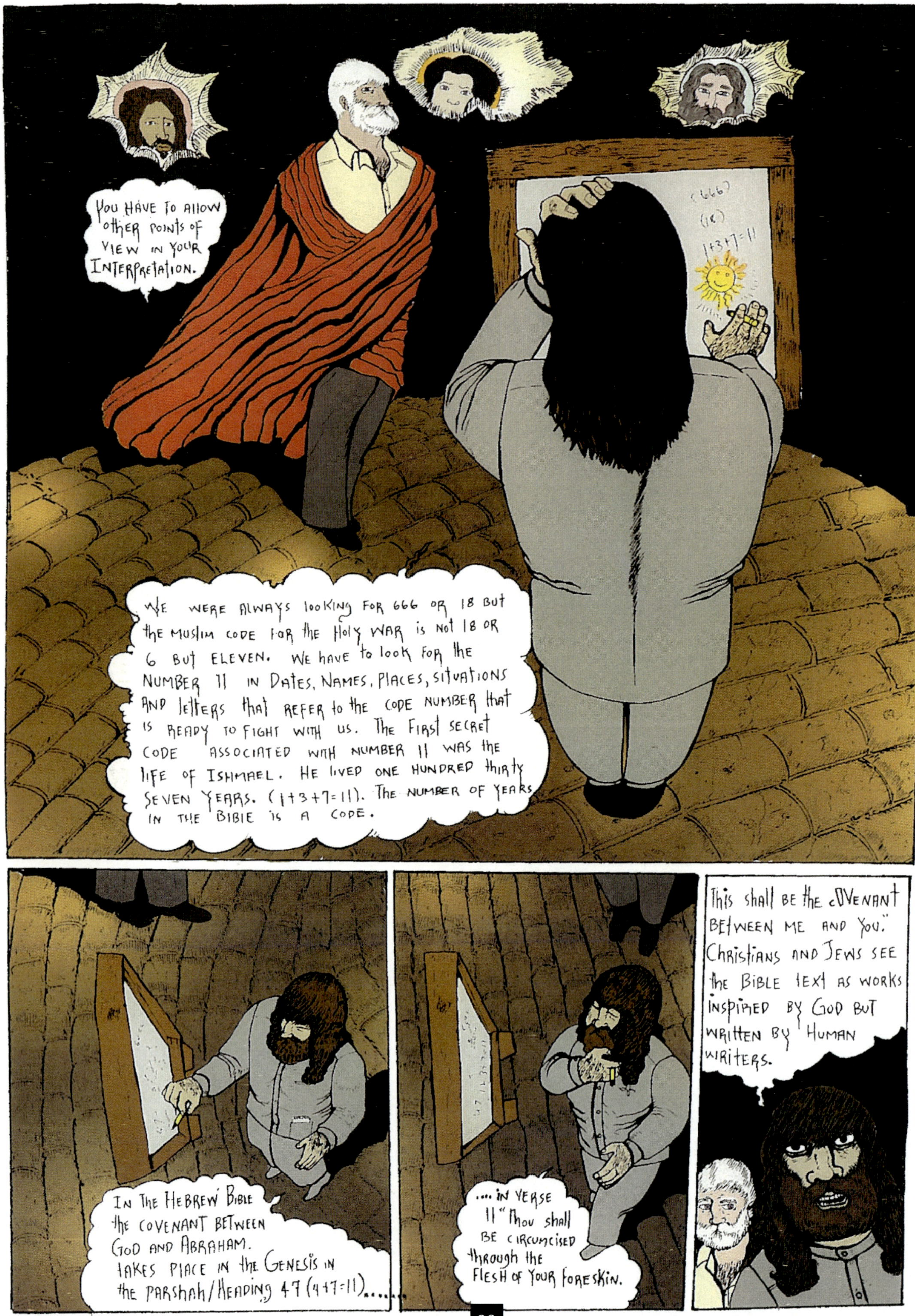

You have to allow other points of view in your interpretation.

(666)
(18)
1+3+7=11

We were always looking for 666 or 18 but the Muslim code for the Holy War is not 18 or 6 but eleven. We have to look for the number 11 in Dates, Names, Places, situations and letters that refer to the code number that is ready to fight with us. The First secret code associated with number 11 was the life of Ishmael. He lived one hundred thirty seven years. (1+3+7=11). The number of years in the Bible is a code.

On the other hand, Muslims believe the Koran is the eternal words of God or Allah Himself. Mohammed is the intermediary of God's words but has nothing to do with the composition of the Koran. It is God's original revelation. The first official compilation of the Koran was made in 650 (6+5=11). In April 623 (6+2+3=11) the first Mosque was finished.
Father, are you losing it? Why number 11?!!
Number 11 can be positive or negative, depending on the way it was used.
Number 11 is exactly half of the powerful number 22. In the beginning the light of the universe was divided into 22 different forces in order to create the universe.
There are twenty-two chromosomes in the human body, plus one that determines a person's sex.
Father, I don't think what you say makes any sense.... its alarmingly quite disturbing.
Yes doctor, twenty-two.

Twenty-two years lasted the revelation to Mohammed. There are twenty-two Arab States in the World. They comprise the Arab league. Mohammed started his emigration from Mecca to Medina in 622, twenty-two again and following that he started with another six, the Anno Hegirae, the Year of the Hegira , really 623. 6+2+3=11. Mohammed died in 632 (6+3+2=11) of the Christian era but this 632 after Christ is exactly the 11th year after the Hegira or the eleventh year in the Muslim Calendar.
Then we have Christian time 6+3+2=11. Muslim time 11. Eleven versus eleven for a total of twenty-two.
Father, I'm really not sure about all your numbers.

The Year Mohammed started teaching the Koran was the Year 614. 6+1+4=11. Muslims Believe that the Koran is the Revelation from God. It is A Revelation that goes exactly against our Christian Revelation. The Revelation of the Godspell against the Revelation of the Koran.
The most powerful number eleven code for the Muslims is Allahu Akbar which is 11 Letters. that is Translates to "God is most Great," but powerful Radical Islamics believe that Allah is the only God, and the rest of us are infidels and should be killed. They believe in the Holy War of God.
The opening verses of Chapter 74, 7+4=11, of the Koran are generally recognized as the oldest of the Revelations given to Mohammed. Why were the oldest & the first revelations placed in Chapter 74, 7+4=11, instead of Chapter One?

I'm not quite..... sure,....

..But I believe in the Koran the longer Shurahs or chapters are placed first regardless of their date.

Doctor, Muslims believe that there are two periods of 11 years in which the Koran was recited to Mohammed, from 610 to 621 in Mecca and from 622 to 632 in Medina and back to Mecca.

The final eleven years are mainly the recitation of old stories of the Bible explained again and again but in opposition to the Christian belief.

The year the Muslims started the expansion and conquest of Europe was the year 711, the number 4 of the Apocalypses again, plus the number 11 again, when the Muslim troops crossed the Strait of Gibraltar and rapidly overran Spain. They immediately changed the name of the mountain to "The Mountain of Tarik" or "Chabad Tarik" which has 11 letters.

They tried to penetrate Europe but were turned back at Poitiers in the year 732. That was just exactly one hundred years after the death of Mohammed and the beginning of the expansion. In the year 641, 6+4+1=11, they conquered Egypt.

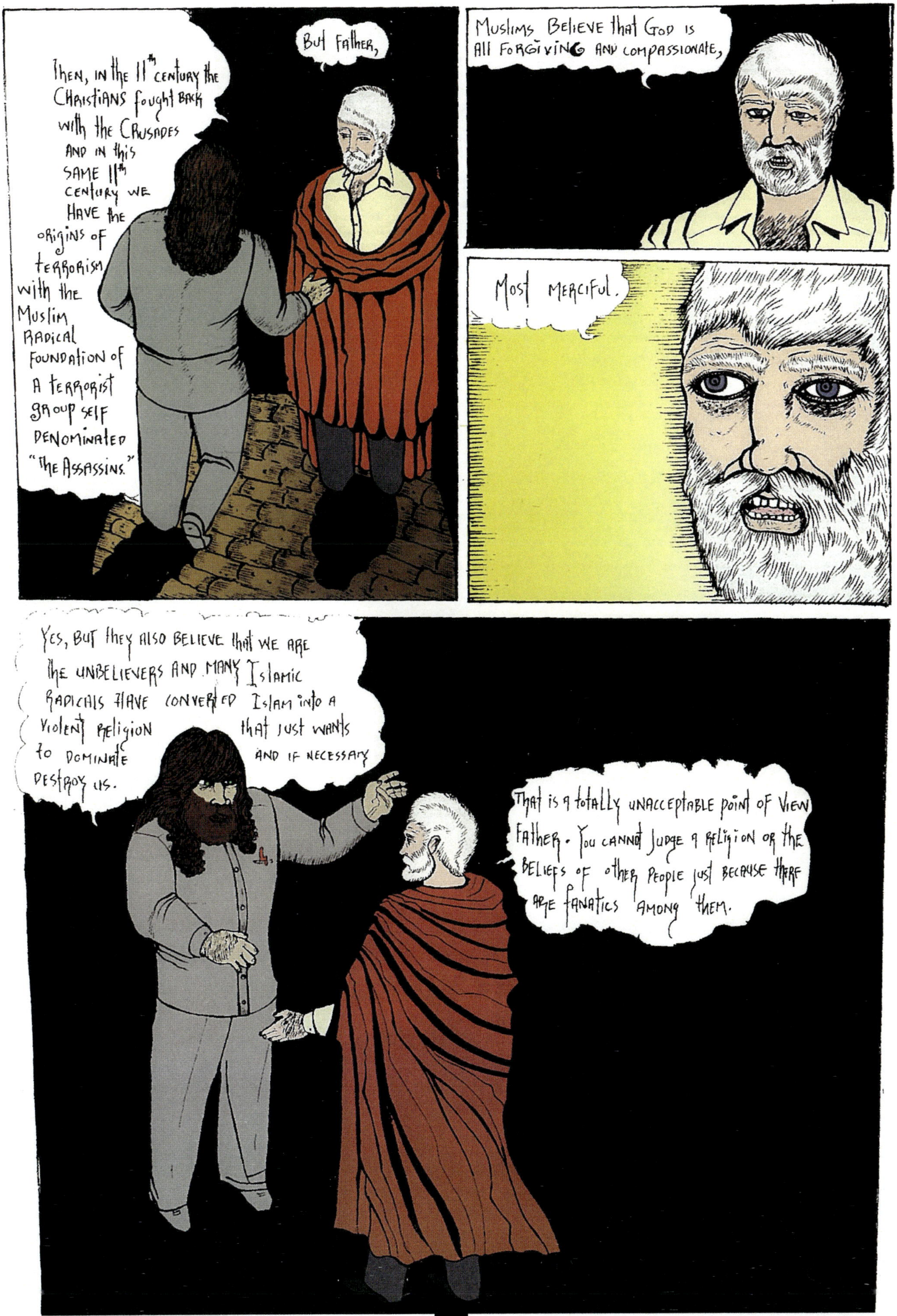

Yes, but they also believe that we are the unbelievers and many Islamic Radicals have converted Islam into a violent Religion that just wants to dominate and if necessary destroy us.

That is a totally unacceptable point of view Father. You cannot judge a religion or the beliefs of other people just because there are fanatics among them.

We are dealing with fanatics, Doctor. They believe that their Book is the only source of truth and final justice. You may try to believe that Islam is a religion of peace, love and justice, but you know as well as I know that you are just pretending. To argue that only a bunch of Islamic fanatics are guilty rather than Islam itself is like arguing that only some German Nazi fanatics were responsible for the murder of 6 million Jews, not the Nazi philosophy itself, or to argue that only a few Communist fanatics under Stalin were responsible for the murder of 20 million people and not the Communist philosophy itself.

I insist Father we must not condemn all Muslims for the actions and crimes of a few.

It is not just the actions of a few. Islam is a harmful religion with a tremendous negative impact on individuals and on the whole society

For Muslims, peace equals submission.

They BELIEVE the whole WORLD should convert to Islam OR BE EXTERMINATED.
IN the ISLAMIC SCHOOLS ALL AROUND the WORLD KIDS LEARN ONLY ABOUT THE KORAN. MATH, SCIENCE, OR LITERATURE ARE SECONDARY. KIDS GROW UP HATING US.
They HATE US BECAUSE they ARE NOT FREE AND WE LOVE FREEDOM. THEY GROW UP with HATE IN their HEARTS, therefore ISLAM IS NO MORE than A MANDATE FOR WAR. I would like to BRING to YOUR ATTENTION SURAH 4, 74. "Let those who Fight IN the CAUSE of Allah who SACRIFICE the life of this world for the HEREAFTER.
To HIM WHO Fights in the CAUSE OF ALLAH, whether HE IS SLAIN OR gets victory, soon shall WE give HIM A 'REWARD OF great VALUE.' Tell ME Doctor. What doctRINE could have BEEN DEVISED MORE CALCULATED TO go FORWARD, IN A BRUTAL CAREER OF CONQUEST, TO BE Followed BY A SET OF IGNORANT AND PREDATORY SOLDIERS than this ASSURANCE of Booty if they SURVIVED OR PARADISE if they FELL?

You are full of Hate, Father!
Christianism promotes peace by the examples of Christ. Islam promotes war by the example of Mohammed. Christ never fought his enemies. Mohammed fought his enemies until he subdued all of them. Christ was killed by his enemies. Mohammed killed his enemies. Christ looked for redemption and forgiveness for his enemies. Mohammed looked for submission or death of his enemies. Christ believed in the equality of men and women. Many Muslims believe that women have no souls & the only way they could attain heaven is only through marriage.
Some Muslim scholars believe that women are at the same level as that of the animals and that is the way they are treated in some Muslim Countries;... Doctor.

I heard that theory before Father and for what I know this misunderstanding arises from Mohammed omitting to mention the enjoyment of women in a future state, but the whole issue is not substantiated by the words or the attitude of Mohammed during his lifetime.

You can believe whatever you want Doctor but you cannot deny the fact that Islamic Extremists truly believe that we are evil. They claim that we are unaware of their realities and this is why radical terrorists believe that God is only with them, and God is the best plotter. This is written in the chapter 8:30 (8+3+0=11) of the Koran. Don't you see, Doctor, that they strongly believe that God is plotting with them against us.

Islamic rulers believe that Islam is the superior, the greatest of all the religions and must always be so. They believe that their faith should be spread all over the world. They believe they have a special obligation to defend Islam with violence if necessary. Radicals strive in the cause of Allah & that will include killing and being killed in his way.

You should become more familiar with the Koran, Doctor. It says "Slay them whenever you may come upon them, and drive them away from wherever they drove you away. Fight against them until there is no more oppression and all worship is devoted to Allah alone." The rule of Allah should apply everywhere and we either convert to Islam or we will be exterminated.

Father, your thoughts are surrounding us with hate.
Saudis are the caretakers of Islam's two holiest sites in Mecca and Medina. The rulers of Saudi Arabia have banned non-believers, known as infidels from stepping into the cities. Whoever backs the infidels against Muslims is considered an infidel.
Islamic government has historically tended to be dominated by a one-man rule and Islam makes no distinction between law and religion. The prophecies of the Book of Daniel are fulfilled here. They believe if you are a Muslim and you abstain from saying your prayers from negligence you should be asked three times to repent.

If you repent all is well, but if you refuse to do it, it is lawful to put you to death. That is the kind of law that the Anti-Christ wants to impose on us.

In the Sura 9, Verse 29 (2+9=11) the Koran specifies what Muslims should do with Christians and Jews: 'Fight those who do not believe in Allah nor the last day, nor hold that

forbidden which has been forbidden by Allah and His Messenger, nor acknowledge the Religion of Truth, even if they are the People of the Book,

until they pay the Jizya (tax) with willing submission and feel themselves subdued.'

It is total submission or destruction. In Surah 5-51 you can read "You who believe, do not take Jews and Christians for your friends and protectors. They are only friends and protectors to each other."

Doctor, 5+5+1=11. They want to impose the Holy War in the way of God.

They Believe that God will make.......... them victorious over the whole world and it is God's rightful command to put all the infidels to Death. The night of faith will last for 6000 years.

Father, I am appalled at what you are saying. Do you really believe your own words?

Dr. Camote, they are taking us over. Can you tell me one Muslim country in the world that is democratic and free? Can you tell me of any single conflict in the world that is not inspired by the Hate of Muslims looking for a Holy War?

Radical Fundamentalist Islamic Groups seek to replace moderate governments with strong fundamentalist regimes in Bosnia, Chechnya, Algeria, Egypt, Sudan, and in many other... countries as well and all over Europe radical Islamists are planting their bases and that will lead us to the final battle.

The battle of.... Armageddon.

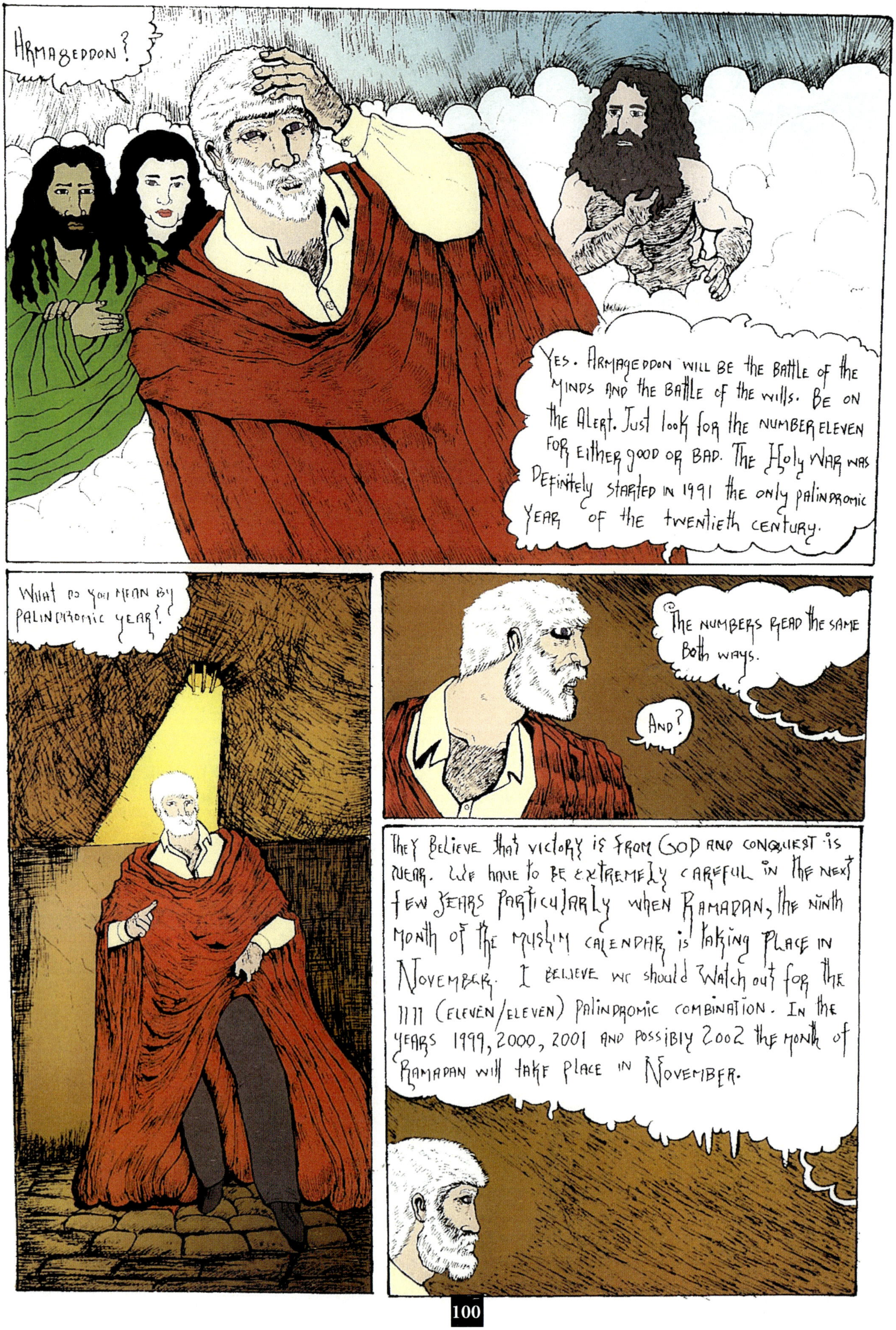

Armageddon?

Yes. Armageddon will be the battle of the minds and the battle of the wills. Be on the alert. Just look for the number eleven for either good or bad. The Holy War was definitely started in 1991 the only palindromic year of the twentieth century.

They believe that victory is from GOD and conquest is near. We have to be extremely careful in the next few years particularly when Ramadan, the ninth month of the Muslim calendar, is taking place in November. I believe we should watch out for the 1111 (eleven/eleven) palindromic combination. In the years 1999, 2000, 2001 and possibly 2002 the month of Ramadan will take place in November.

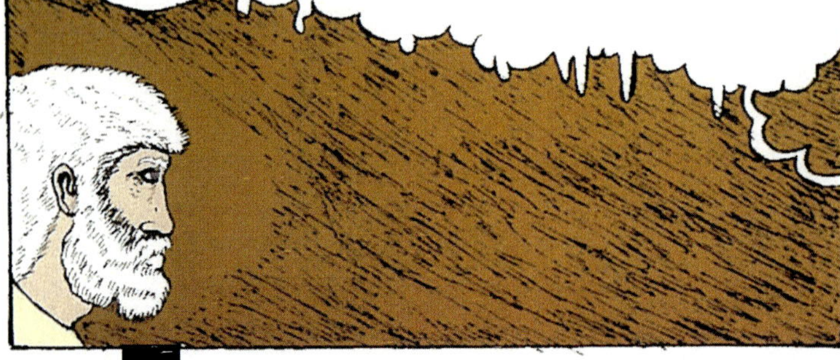

I believe that in the year 2001 of our Christian era the month of Ramadan will start around November 11 (11/11).

The Revelation states 'Small and Great, Both Rich and Poor, Both Free and Slaves.' That is exactly the Ramadan. The month in which every Muslim becomes equal. The holy war was definitely started in 1991. Everything started in the palindromic year of 1991.

How long do you think the Holy War will last?

The first part of this Holy War will last for another eleven years until we reach the next palindromic year. That will be the year 2002, which is the only palindromic year in the twenty-first century. There are eleven years between the two palindromic years, 1991 to 2002. The next palindromic year will be in 110 more years, in the year 2112. The last time that eleven years lasted between two palinromic years was eleven centuries ago from 898 to 909. And don't forget Dr. Camote, that the most perfect palindromic year since the beginning of Christianity and since the beginning of Islam is the year 1111.

But Father we are in the year 1995.

Yes but for the Muslims it is the year 1415, 1+4+1+5=11.

The code 11 is connected in four ways that I know to the palindromic 11 year period.

The first I already mentioned to you is the Muslim year 1415. 1+4+1+5=11. They are preparing something big right now.
The second was when the number of Islamic countries in the four corners of the earth joined the Organization of the Islamic Conference and reached 56 countries. 5+6=11. This is the exact number of countries right now.
The third fact will be when 47 (4+7=11) nations in the world will have a majority of Muslim population. This is a new fact today.
The fourth fact is that this year the number of Muslims all over the world reached the number of 1.1 Billion. There is the number 11 once again. Eleven hundred million Muslims.

You make no sense Father.....
Do you want to hear more, Doctor?

YEAH, SURE ...... why Not?
The world population will be around six billion people in just a couple of years.
Around the year 2000 or 2001 the world population will reach 6.4 billion people and the Muslim's population will be over 1.2 billion.
When the total percentage of Muslims all over the world represents 19.91% of the world population they will strike.
Why 19.91%?
Palindromic Year 1991 meets Palindromic 19.91%.
The numbers might change in sequence like 1, 9, 1, 11, 9, 1, 19, 11 and so on. This is the countdown of the final battle of the Holy War. They will strike in the year 2000 or 2001 or the latest during the year 2002 or 2003. If we do not stop them they will strike back dramatically in the year 2009 or 2011, or within those two years.
Why 2009 or 2011?

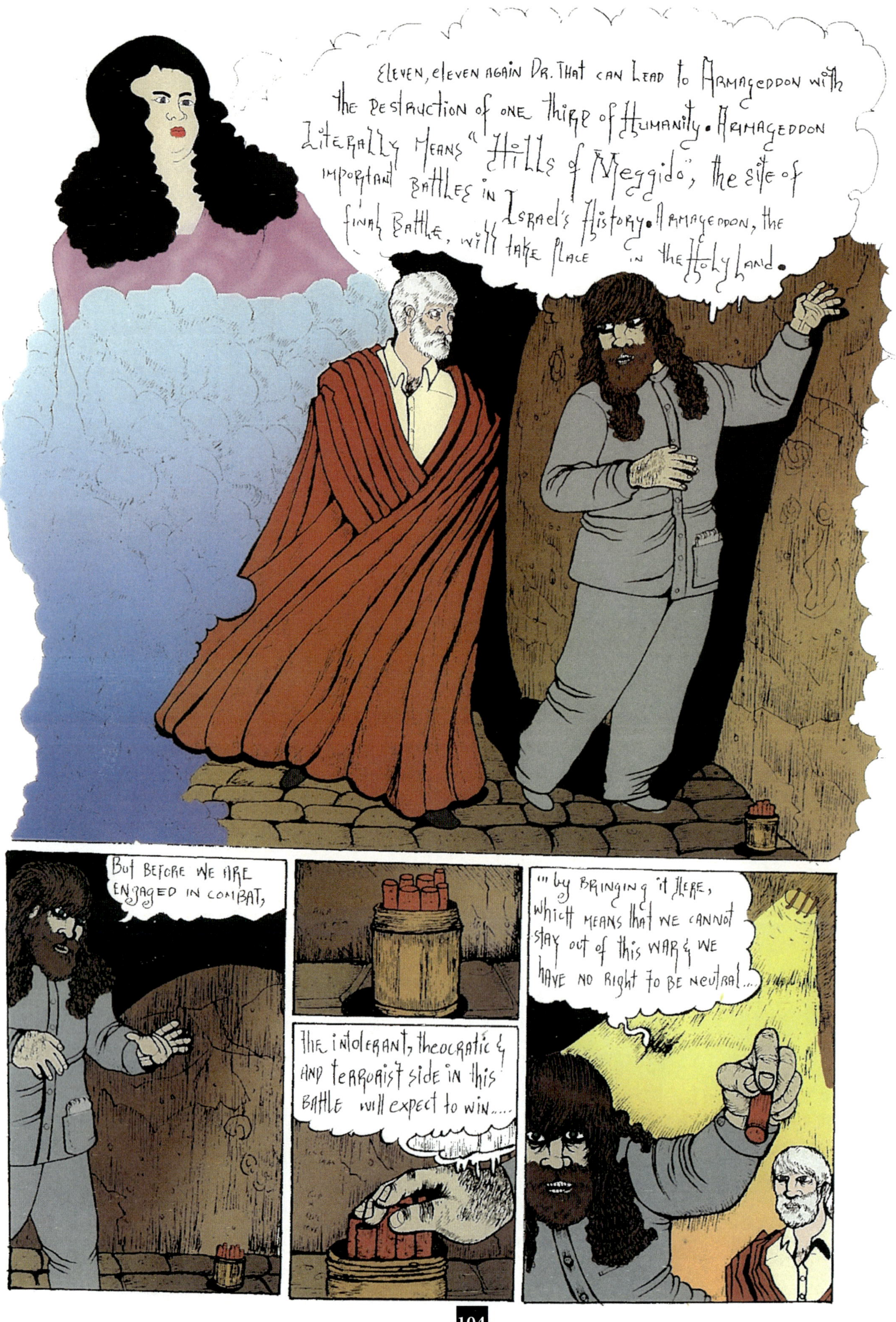

Eleven, eleven again Dr. That can lead to Armageddon with the destruction of one thire of Humanity. Armageddon literally means "Hills of Meggido", the site of important battles in Israel's History. Armageddon, the final battle, will take place in the Holy Land.

It is very hard to believe in prophecies about the Apocalypse.
Oh Doctor, I forgot to mention something else that might be of interest to you.
And that will be?
Dr...are you...ahhh... ..familiar with mirror reading?
Yes! it reads backwards.
According to the Bible mirror reading is the only way to see into the future!!
Do you know the name by which all men, women and children in Mecca knew the Prophet?
No, I don't.
Al-Amin, the trustworthy. Do you read Hebrew or Arabic?
Some.

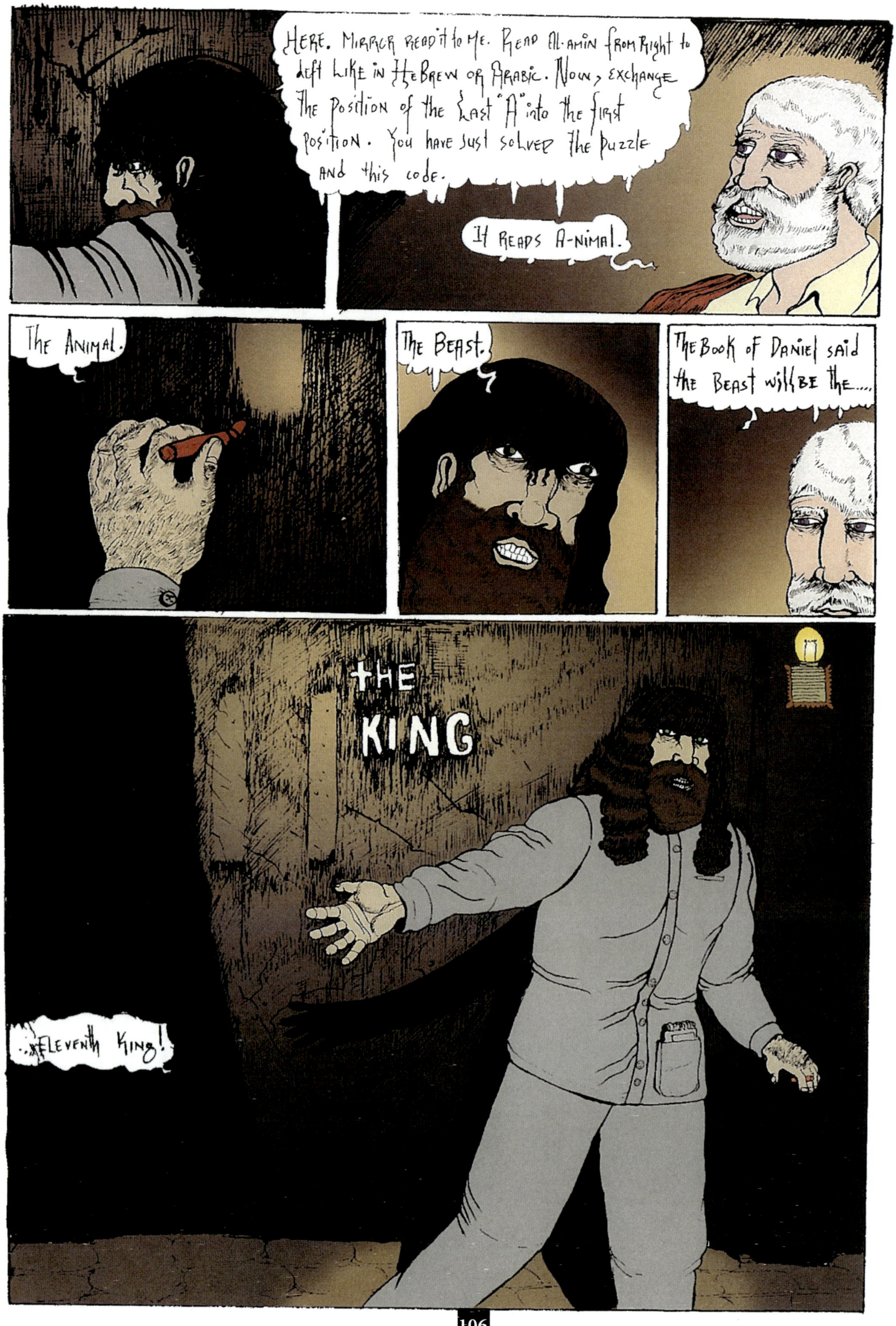

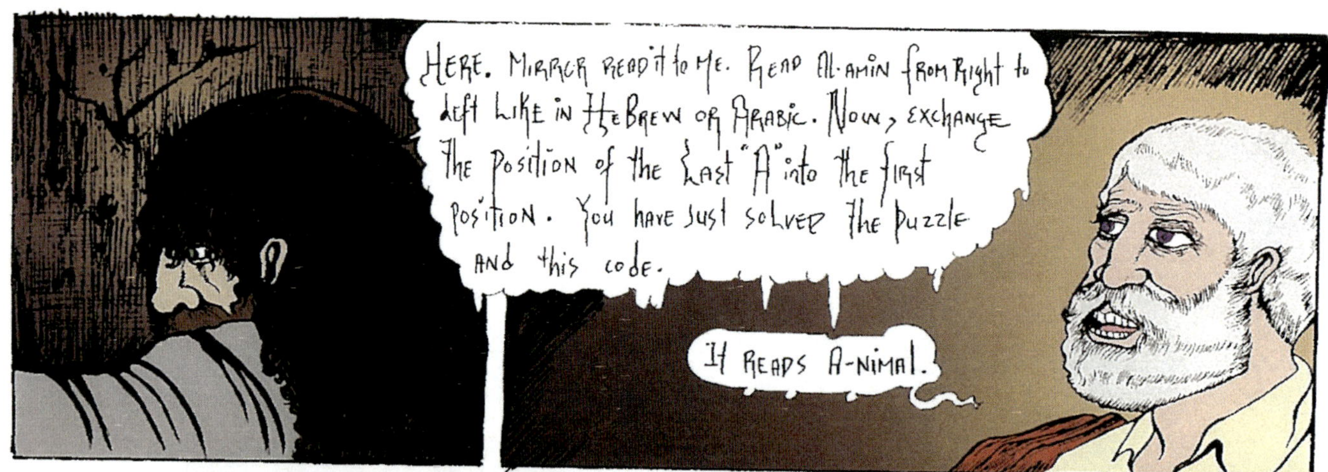

the
KING

...Eleventh King!

I SENT MY psychiatric Evaluation of Him to the Authorities, He Remains A Haunting MEMORY To ME.
HE WAS A MAN FILLED with PARANOIA AND Hate I NEVER SAW HIM AGAIN.
Extremism CAN BE DESTRUCTIVE FOR AN INDIVIDUAL OR FOR ALL MANKIND. The Anti-Christ IS A CODE AND it CAN BE IDENTIFIED with multiple PROBLEMS in the WORLD. What Do you think?
I DO NOT BELIEVE that ANY Religion IS SUPERIOR TO ANY OTHER, AND EVENTUALLY AT SOME TIME IN the ENDLESS CYCLE OF OUR REINCARNATED LIVES WE WILL BE PART OF ALL RELIGIONS. WE ARE LINKED IN the JOURNEY OF LIFE. IN SOME FUTURE EXISTENCE I MIGHT CHANGE PLACES, AND I MIGHT BE BORN AGAIN AS A Muslim living in Morocco OR Saudi Arabia, AND A Muslim from Saudi Arabia may BE REBORN AS A JEW living IN New York, Miami OR JERUSALEM. The IMPORTANT thing to REMEMBER IS WE ARE ALL THE SAME, REGARDLESS OF OUR RACE, GENDER OR WHERE WE RESIDE. Everything is TRANSIENT AND SUBJECT TO CHANGE.

Evil spirits can take over Religious extremists and terrorists of any Religion to inflict pain on people and in countries. Those people who say that their God is the only God are acting against God because they are imposing their Beliefs on others by any means possible.
Sebastian, every time you go into the world the main purpose is to change your nature. Past, present and future are always with you. When you come back to the world you bring your baggage from previous lifetimes. Sebastian, sometimes the baggage is too heavy.

What do you MEAN?

In the Beginning all the souls agreed in going through a learning experience.

We agreed to change places, religions, genders but through successive reincarnations many souls are forgetting their true nature and they want to reincarnate as soon as possible. They just try to get the first available body of the same race and within the most familiar country.

The original experiment has been forgotten. The baggage is too heavy and the emotions too strong to have a conscious selection of the next reincarnation.

Today, not enough souls are choosing their parents and their objectives. The majority of the souls are going back into the battlefield really fast and just looking for revenge.

They go back to Earth and they are immediately disconnected from the Light.

Is that the reason why there is so much hate in the world?
Yes.

Hate is not fully discarded in the afterlife. The learning place is more like the waiting place.

Just a place to find a new body to go back to Earth. Emotions are running high in the afterlife.

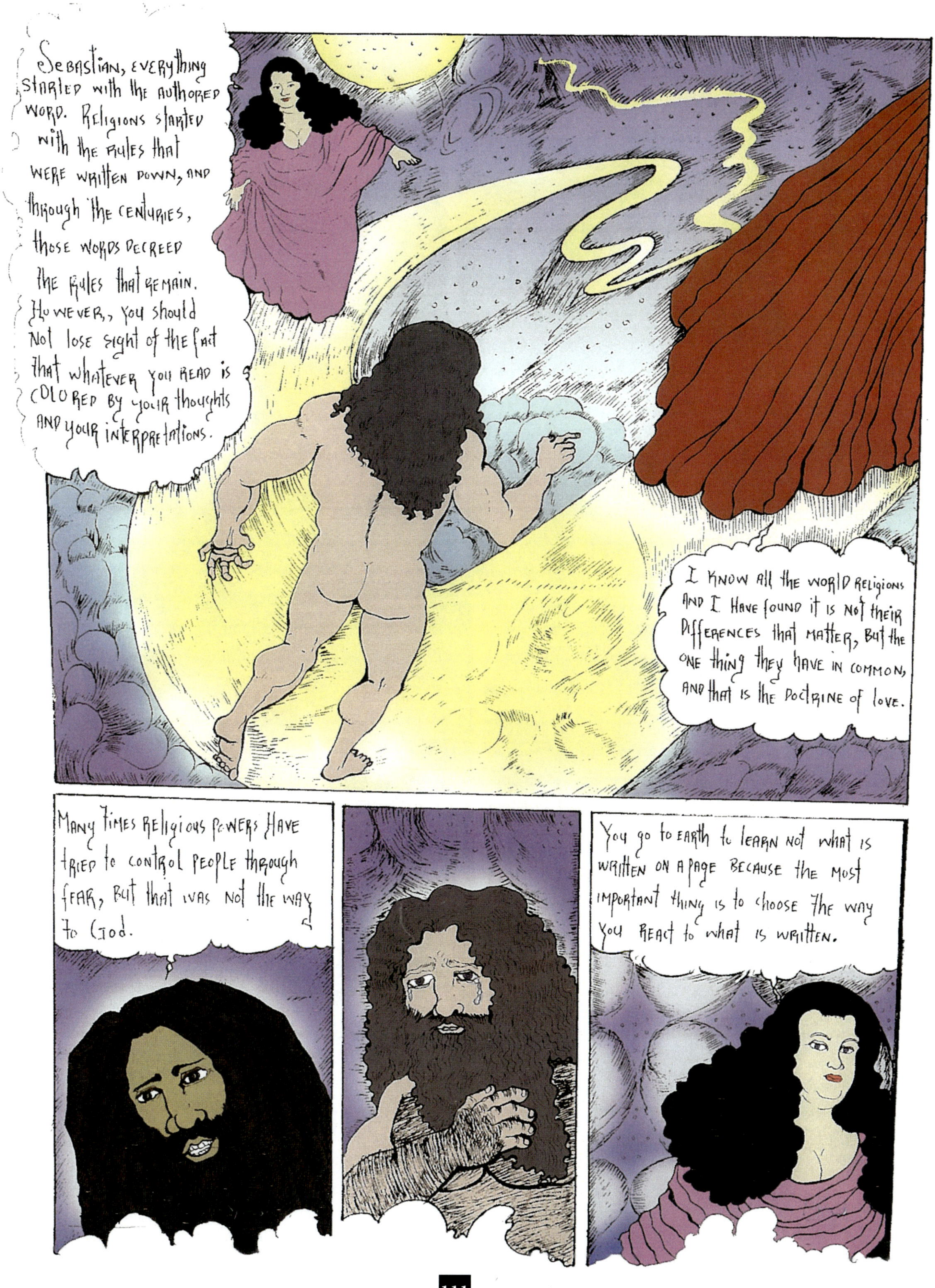

Sebastian, everything started with the authored word. Religions started with the rules that were written down, and through the centuries, those words decreed the rules that remain. However, you should not lose sight of the fact that whatever you read is colored by your thoughts and your interpretations.

I know all the world religions and I have found it is not their differences that matter, but the one thing they have in common, and that is the doctrine of love.

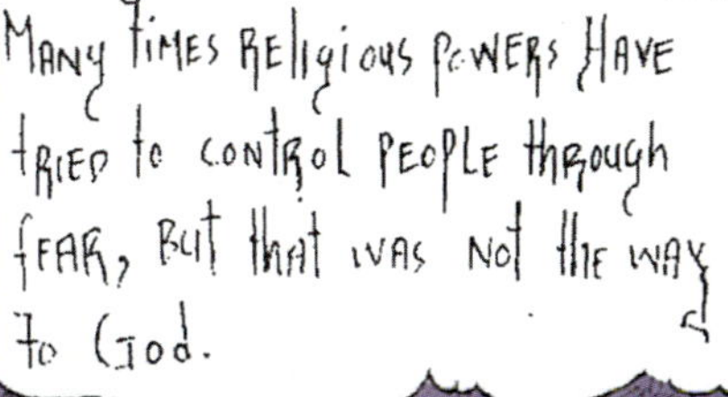

You go to earth to learn not what is written on a page because the most important thing is to choose the way you react to what is written.

Whatever Religion you choose to study or Practice will lead to your spirituality. All spiritual paths lead to love and kindness and will help you to reunite you and be one with God. Remember, Sebastian, everything is intent.
Intent?
If you have good intentions the universe will support your dreams and desires.
Yes, Sebastian, what you need to do is to banish doubts from your mind.

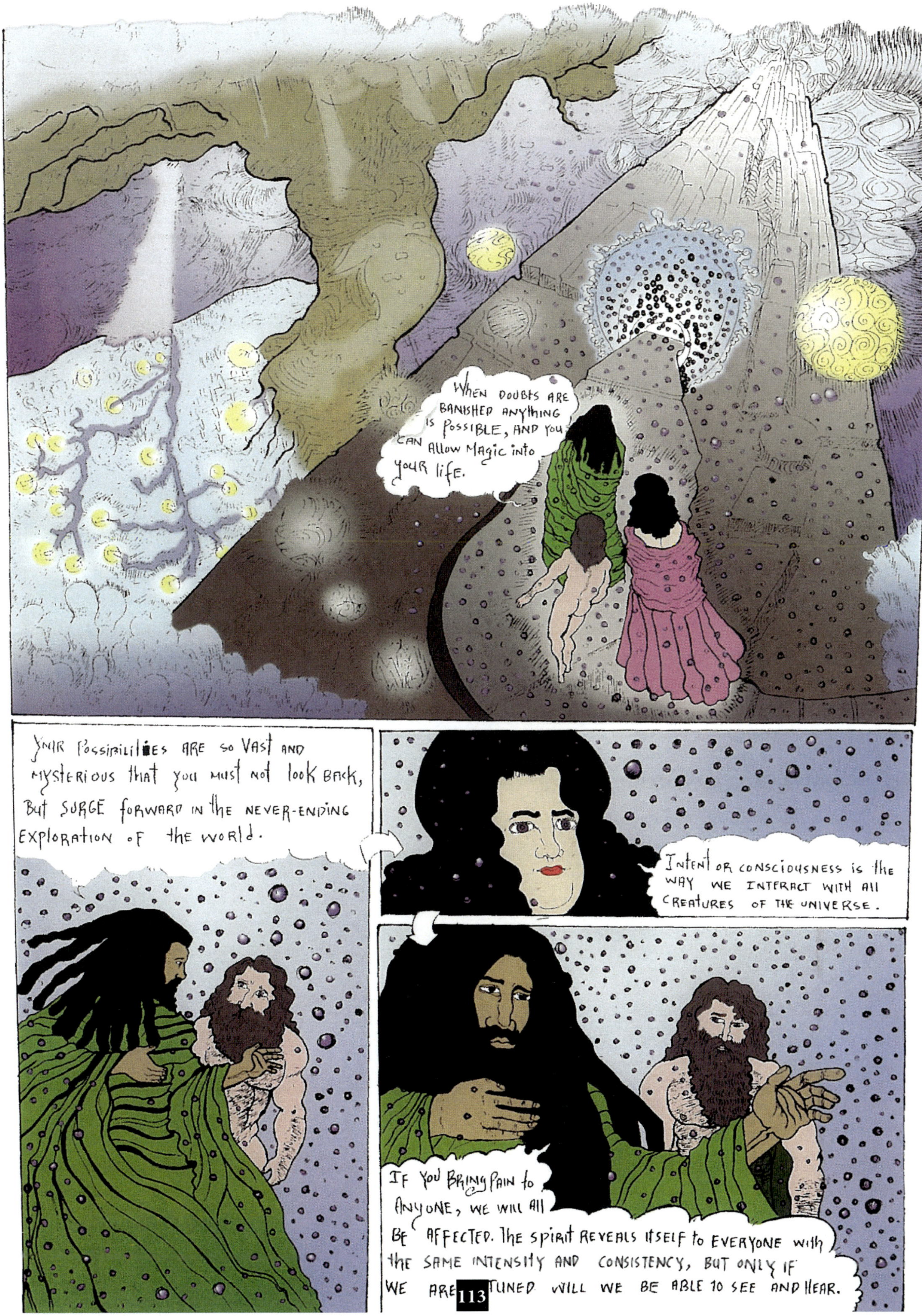

When doubts are banished anything is possible, and you can allow magic into your life.

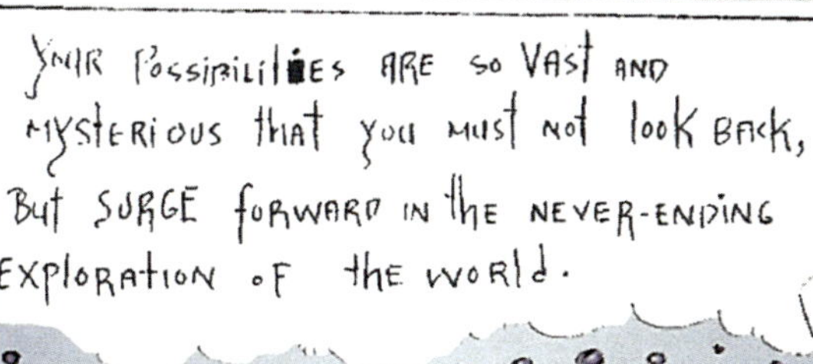

As long as you feel you are the most important thing in the world, you will not be able to appreciate the wonders of the things around you.
We are all part of the universe and we each have our own mission.
Never feel you are more important in the scheme of life than the merit of a tiny ant.
The sun will continue to rise and set without you, ...
... even after you are gone.

Your final statement Sebastian!

Could it have happened differently? Was that fateful night my destiny?

Where were you?
Commodore Plaza.

Alone?
LOVE LIVES!

I was walking with Camotin. It was Halloween.

What were you wearing?

I was dressed in my Cosmic Knight costume carrying my sword.

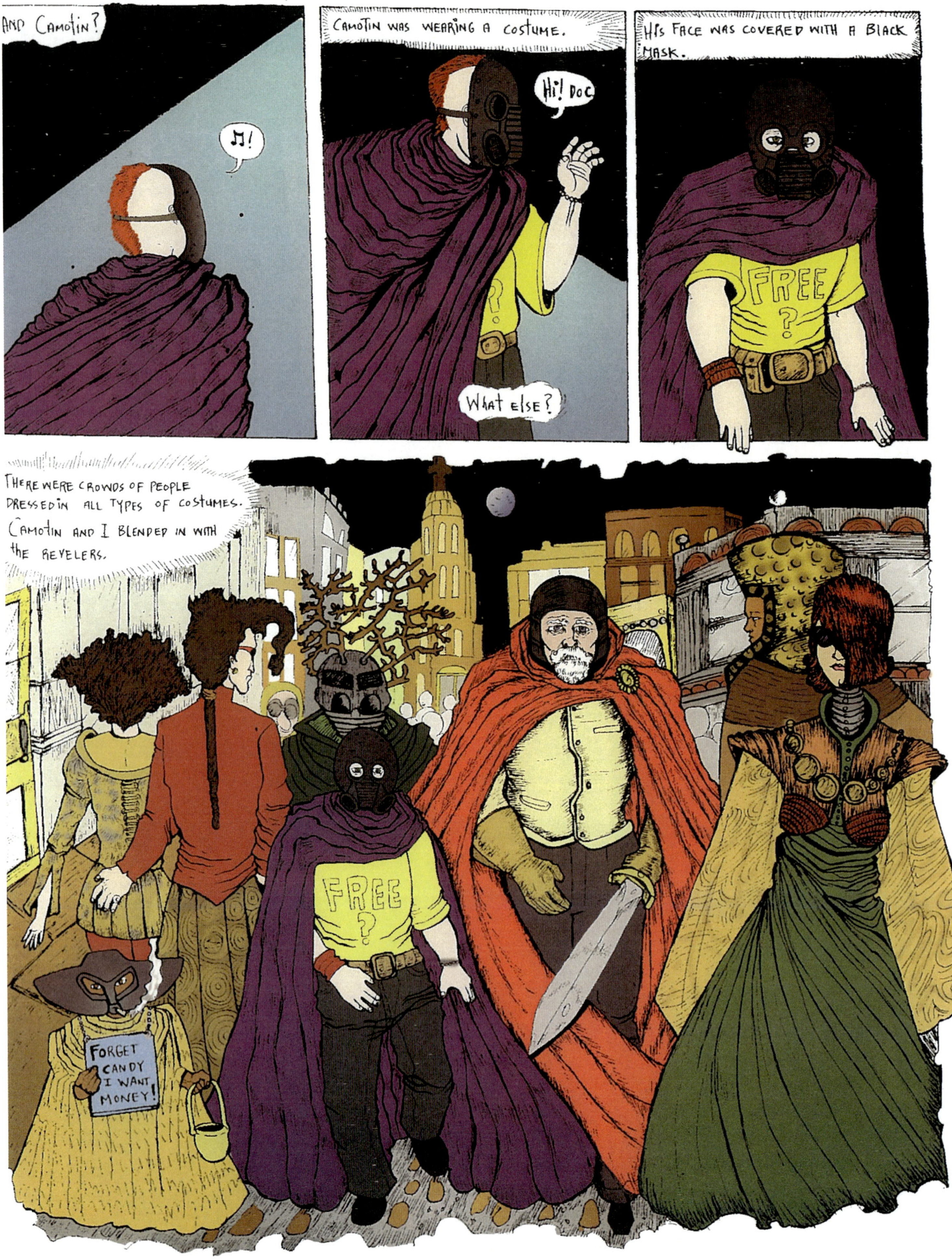

THERE WERE CROWDS OF PEOPLE DRESSED IN ALL TYPES OF COSTUMES. CAMOTIN AND I BLENDED IN WITH THE REVELERS.

FREE ?

FORGET CANDY I WANT MONEY!

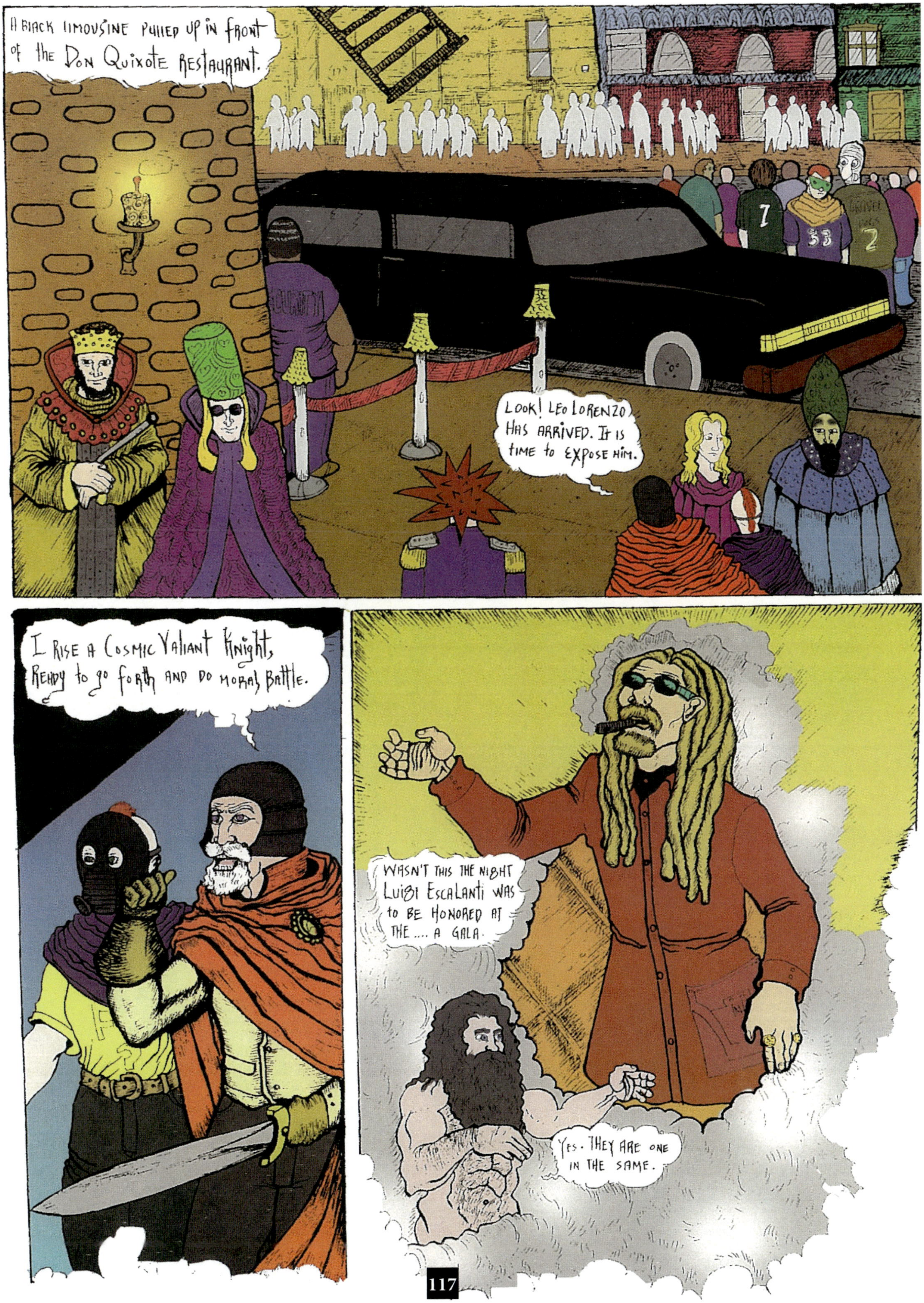

A BLACK LIMOUSINE PULLED UP IN FRONT OF THE DON QUIXOTE RESTAURANT.

LOOK! LEO LORENZO HAS ARRIVED. IT IS TIME TO EXPOSE HIM.

There was a huge inflated plastic giant anchored on top of the windmill in the front of the Restaurant in honor of Halloween.
Yes, I remember. The wind started to blow. The windmill to spin and.......
And Lorenzo looked up at the huge inflated giant leaping and plunging up in the air. And watched you do what Dr. Camote?
I fought the giant!
And what was he doing then, Dr. Camote?

Laughing.
HA HA HA HA HA HA HA HA HA HA HA HA
Laughing at who?
He was laughing at me.
And this made you even more outraged. Didn't it, Dr. Camote?
Coward! Criminal evil alien! A real Cosmic Knight is ready to fight you. I command myself to my beautiful lady Dulcinea, with all my heart. Defend yourself, coward.

50
HIP-HOP LIVES
LOVE
WHO is this idiot? Is this some Kind of Joke?
I AM A COSMIC KNIGHT!
BE CAREFUL, CRAZY ONE. I MIGHT SHOOT YOUR..... HEAD OFF.
AND THEN WHAT HAPPENED?
ESCALANTI!......LORENZO..!

Escalanti grabs Lucy and pulls her in front of him as a human shield

Lucy's gun is fired in the air.

Dr. Camote charges, yelling....

..and thrust his sword into the woman's body.
I went into shock when I realized.....

Camotin reached down and took off her mask.

Who was she Sebastain?
What have I done?

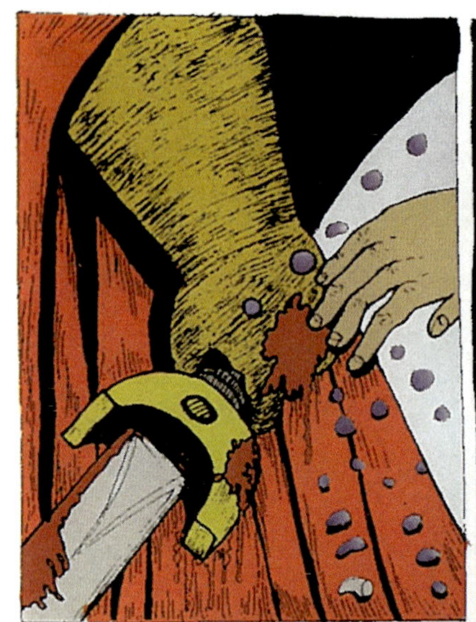

It was not only a woman in costume that your sword thrust into that night, was it Dr. Camote?

I am naked in the searchlight of truth.

It was Lucy Neal you killed that night.
Never did I realize the extent of pain there is in the world. My lady, forgive me. I cannot bear the thought that I have lost you forever through my fault. I love you with my heart and soul.
I.... hear every throb of your life, every sorrow, every joy fading and neither the angels in heaven nor the demons in the sea will ever dissever the soul of Don Quixote from the soul of my beautiful Dulcinea.
It is said everyone must endure grief at some point in a lifetime, and he who cries today will laugh tomorrow.
Lucy did not believe that.

LIFE CAN CHANGE IN AN INSTANT.
WHO CAN EVER FORESEE THE MOMENT WHEN THE LIFE OF A CHILD MIGHT BE GONE. LUCY BELIEVED IT WAS LUIGI ESCALANTI'S FAULT THAT MICHAEL WAS DEAD. BUT THAT WAS NEVER PROVEN. WHEN LUCY NEAL BOUGHT THE GUN FROM CAMOTIN.
IT WAS CAMOTIN, MY FRIEND THAT GAVE HER THE GUN?
YES, SEBASTIAN. SHE INTENDED TO USE IT TO FATALLY SHOOT LUIGI ESCALANTI.

Camotin was then a Part of our Destiny.
Lucy went to you, Dr. Camote for Help,
But...
...You Allowed Your fantasy to Become more important.
I Killed Her and I Killed myself. There is no injustice. My Pain is my Destiny. Life is a Dream. Dulcinea is Always with Me. She is my Soul. Our Love is Everlasting, lifetime after lifetime. Why are we so fond of a life that Begins with a cry and ends with a Groan?
You Have come here to clarify the events of your life,......
...to comprehend your mistakes and to see, that circumstances on Earth are not always as they appear to be. You cannot know the many riddles and mysteries of the universe when you are Earthbound.
There are victories and defeats for every Human Being.
Now Sebastian, you are going to meet the Light.

AFTER you MEET The light you will ENTER ANOTHER PHASE.

It will be important that you do not take earthly concerns with you.

YOU MUST CONCENTRATE ON
the white light, ...

.... AND love, love VERY DEEPly.

CONCENTRATE...... CONCENTRATE

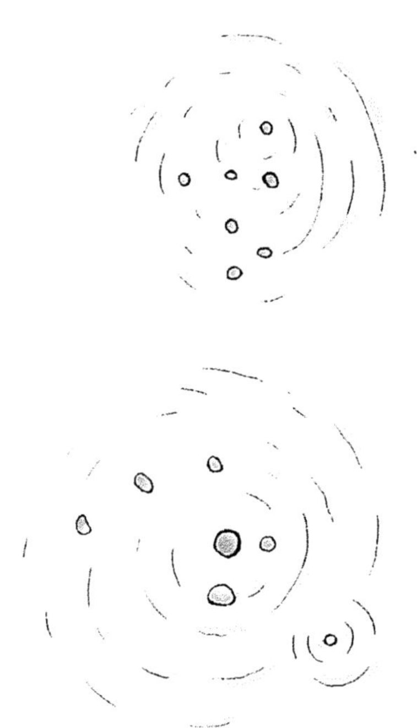

Made in the USA
Monee, IL
13 August 2025

23048478R00081